# THE REPRISAL

# THE REPRISAL

## THE ELIMINATOR SERIES BOOK 3

### MIKE RYAN

WWW.MIKERYANBOOKS.COM

# 1

J acobs was hanging around in Eddie's Pawn Shop for a few hours as he often seemed to do. For some strange reason that neither man could quite put their finger on, they actually were becoming friends. Jacobs found himself at the pawn shop, if not every day, at least four or five times a week. Maybe it was the boredom that was getting to him. He didn't really have anything else to do other than training Gunner. But he couldn't do that twelve hours a day. He didn't want to overwork Gunner, so he tried to limit the training to a couple hours a day with some breaks sprinkled in between.

It'd been several weeks since his conversation at the prison with Mallette and there hadn't been a single incident since then. It appeared the two men had a truce. At least for the time being. But it also seemed to leave Jacobs with a void that he appeared to have trouble filling with anything else. He lacked a purpose.

It was mid-afternoon and Jacobs was hanging in the back office as Franks was tending to a customer out front. As he waited, he did a few basic commands with Gunner and gave him a treat as he sat. After a few minutes, Franks finished with his customer and came walking into the back.

"Making yourself at home?" Franks asked.

"Sure am. Must be pretty awkward having to deal with a customer and all since it happens so infrequently."

"Ha ha, very funny. I have just the right number of customers that I need. If I get any more than that, then I'll actually have to do work here and actually operate like a real business."

"Yeah. Who needs that?" Jacobs said, giving Gunner another treat.

"Hey, I was thinking about visiting Lucy and Deb at the massage place after work. Feel like coming?"

It didn't take Jacobs long to respond. "Nah. I'll just do some stuff at home."

"You need to get out of your doldrums, my friend."

"I'm not in any doldrums."

"I beg to differ. Ever since that meeting with Mallette, you've been looking like you're down in the dumps."

Jacobs shook his head, not wanting to acknowledge it. "I'm not."

"Why don't you just take out the rest of his men?" Franks asked. "You're being very trusting of a man who's tried to kill you and has killed members of your family."

"Don't wanna risk it. If I take out a few more of his men, I don't wanna risk him retaliating against my brother and his family, or even Val's parents."

"You really think you can trust him?"

Jacobs threw his hands up. "He's living up to it so far."

"So, you're just gonna wait ten years until he's out of prison before continuing your war?"

Jacobs shrugged.

"How do you know he's not just planning something against you right now? How do you know he's not putting together some grand, magnificent plan to take out your brother, your wife's parents, and you all at the same time? He's capable of it, you know."

"I know. But what do you want me to do?" Jacobs asked.

"I don't necessarily want you to do anything. I'm just trying to make sure you know that you're playing by rules that he might not be. Just because things are silent doesn't mean you should let your guard down."

Jacobs just looked at him for a minute. Franks was right. Jacobs hadn't done much of anything the last couple of weeks except sitting around. He stopped gathering intelligence, stopped keeping tabs on Mallette's men, stopped doing everything. And he hated admitting when Franks was right. But there was no doubt he was here. Jacobs needed to get back on the ball. Just in case Mallette was up to something, Jacobs didn't want to be caught with his pants down.

"You sure you don't wanna head to the massage place later?" Franks asked again.

"I'm sure."

"C'mon, man, you need to get back on the horse and ride again."

"Uh, no, I don't."

"You'll be able to take a load off and de-stress."

"I'm fine," Jacobs said.

"You take Lucy, I'll take Deb. You look like more of a Lucy guy. I prefer Deb anyway. She's a little bit wilder if you know what I mean."

"Uh, yep, I know what you mean."

"Besides, I think Lucy is kind of sweet on you."

Jacobs shook his head, not really interested in any part of the conversation. "I'm good."

"Why not?"

Jacobs didn't have much of a reason except that he didn't want to. Part of it was that he still considered himself attached to Valerie. He couldn't see himself with anyone else, even for a night. "I dunno. I guess because I'm still married."

"But you're not."

"But I feel like I am."

"Except that you're not," Franks said.

"But I am."

"OK. Except that you're not."

"Are we just gonna continue to do this Laurel and Hardy routine?" Jacobs asked.

"Who?"

Jacobs shook his head. "Never mind."

"Seriously, no disrespect to the former missus, but you gotta move on at some point."

Jacobs glared up at him, not really wanting to hear it. Franks could tell that he seemed a little agitated at the statement and tried to smooth things over.

"I'm just saying," Franks said, putting his arms up. "Move on when you're ready."

"I appreciate your concern," Jacobs replied, remaining calm. "But you don't just forget the love of your life in a few months."

"I'm not saying forget. I'm just saying move on to a new chapter. You can never get back what you had."

"I know that."

"That's all I'm saying. And now I'll stop preaching to you."

Jacobs gave him a fake smile. "I appreciate that too."

After a few more minutes of chat, Jacobs was ready to go home for the night. Before he left, though, Franks had a few more things on his mind.

"So, if this moratorium with Mallette continues, what do you think your other plans will be?"

"Moratorium? Big word. You been reading the dictionary again?"

"Hardy har har. Seriously, though."

"I dunno," Jacobs answered. "Why do you ask?"

"Maybe you should take your talents elsewhere."

Jacobs looked at him strangely, sure he must have had a point in there somewhere. But considering Franks liked to talk in circles sometimes, he wasn't sure he'd get it. "Um... is that supposed to mean something?"

"Means there's a lot of people out there who could use your help."

Jacobs still looked at him like he had two heads. "No idea what you're referring to."

"Like I said, you need a purpose. A reason to keep on going. There's people out there who could use you fighting for them."

"What, like a bodyguard or something?"

"No. Listen, we both know there's people out there who need help. People who slip through the cracks. People who won't go to the police, can't go to the police, or for whatever reason, there's just nothing the cops can do at that point."

"Yeah?"

"They need someone like you," Franks said.

Jacobs had an idea what he was saying but wanted to make it crystal clear. "What exactly are you saying I should do? Hire myself out to these people? Become some kind of vigilante or something? Become some kind of superhero?"

"Hey, you can use whatever kind of term you want.

I'm just saying there's people who could use your talents."

Jacobs scrunched his face together as he thought about it, though the idea wasn't something that initially struck him as something he was interested in pursuing. He didn't quit his job or forge down the path he was on for any other purpose than revenging the murder of his family. Any other good he did while on that mission was just a byproduct of that and not his primary intent.

"No, I don't think so," Jacobs said, shaking his head. "I'm not really interested in helping anyone else."

"You were a cop. Wasn't that your life's work?"

"Was is the key word there. That part of me is gone."

"I don't think it is. It's still there. Maybe buried a little deeper right now, but it's still in there."

"What's gotten into you? What's with this righteous civilian attitude that you got going on right now?" Jacobs asked. "Since when did you care so much about helping others?"

"Hey, I may technically be on the wrong side of the law, but I don't go around hurting people. I might make a quick buck sidestepping the law or skirting around it, but nobody gets hurt."

"That you know of. I'm sure people have been hurt as a result of things you've done, even indirectly."

Franks shrugged. "Maybe so. And maybe I'm just a

hypocrite. I just think, looking at you sitting here before me, helping others would be good for you."

"Well, I'm deeply touched by your genuine level of concern over my well-being," Jacobs said, putting his hand over his heart.

"Fine, fine, make fun if you want to."

Jacobs laughed, not wanting to hurt his feelings. "No, I'm really touched. I am. I'm not trying to tease you or anything. I'll think about it."

"All right. Just trying to give you some career guidance is all."

"And I'll give it some thought. I really will."

With that out of the way, Jacobs left and went home for the night. Though he tried to just spend the night relaxing, he couldn't help but let thoughts of his conversation with Franks enter his mind from time to time. It was one of the few nights where he didn't try to do anything other than watch TV. He'd already spent time training Gunner earlier, so he had nothing else to do. Nothing except think. And the more the thought about it, the more he thought that maybe Franks was on to something. He needed a purpose. Something to drive him. He wasn't a person who liked to wander around aimlessly with nothing to do.

Jacobs gave serious thought to Franks' proposition, wondering if that's what he wanted. He wasn't against helping anyone who needed a hand, but he didn't know where he'd find these people. Would he just wander the streets at night and wait for someone to scream out? He also wondered whether he should just continue his war with Mallette's troops. All was quiet now, but Franks was right, trusting Mallette was a losing game. Jacobs thought that maybe he should finish the job he started out doing.

He also knew that up to this point, he had successfully avoided police operations. He wasn't wanted for anything and he wasn't hiding from them. But Jacobs knew that that could change if he kept up or even expanded his plans. The good thing about taking the fight to Mallette's crew was that he could control the situation. He was on the offensive for the most part and he knew who and what he was dealing with. If he started helping every poor soul that came across his path, that wouldn't always be the case. There would be times when he wasn't sure who his opponent was or what their angle would be. And the more situations he got involved in, the more likely he was to eventually be put on the police radar. He couldn't stay out of the spotlight forever.

Jacobs was so focused on everything that was going through his mind that he didn't even hear his phone ringing at first. It wasn't until Gunner barked that Jacobs finally heard the phone ring. He looked at his watch, and it was after ten. Considering the time, he figured it was likely Franks calling for some reason. Maybe it was to brag about what a good time he had at the massage place without him. Knowing Franks, it could have been just about anything.

"Hope you're not calling to brag," Jacobs said.

"What? No. I could really use your help down here though."

Jacobs scrunched his eyebrows together, not sure what that was supposed to mean. "What could you possibly need my help with? Are you at the massage place?"

"That I am."

"Then I don't see what you need with me. I'm sure you are in very capable hands with Lucy and Deb."

"Well, that's kind of what I wanted to talk to you about," Franks said.

"Listen, Eddie, I appreciate what you're trying to do. But I'm really not interested right now. Maybe in a few months or something."

"No, no, I understand all that. I respect your position, but I need your help with something else. Something important."

Jacobs was at a loss as to what else Franks would need his help with. "What's going on?"

"Is there a way you could come down here? I'd really rather show you in person."

"Show me what?"

"Like I said, if you could meet me here, I can tell you what's going on."

"Are you in some kind of trouble?" Jacobs asked, wondering if one of Franks' former clients was unhappy with one of their deals and caught up with him. "Is someone there?"

"What? No, no, no, nothing like that. There's no trouble, everything's fine, I could really just use your help."

"You realize you sound very creepy right now, right?"

"Do I? I dunno, I'm just trying to figure out the best way to get you down here," Franks said.

"Are you setting me up for something?"

"Do you really think I would do something like that to you?"

"Uh, yeah, I do. It'd be a big mistake, but yeah, I think you would," Jacobs replied.

"Well, I'm not setting you up. I'm not asking you to do anything against your principles. Just need you to look at something and advise me how to proceed."

"I swear if you got me walking into something you're gonna spend the next few months in traction."

"Uh, noted, noted. Just get down here as soon as you can, OK?"

Jacobs hung up and immediately looked over to Gunner. Alarm bells were ringing out in his head as he wondered what he was walking into. Obviously, something was going on. His gut was telling him that Franks was in trouble and being used to get to him. He couldn't think of any other reason as to why Franks would be so intent on having him come down to the massage parlor. As he looked at Gunner, assuming he was walking into danger, Jacobs thought this might be the right time to deploy the dog. His training had been going very well over the past few weeks. Maybe it was time to put that training to the test.

"You ready to go to work?" Jacobs asked. Gunner perked up and looked at him, slightly tilting his head. "Let's do this."

## 2

As Jacobs approached the massage parlor, he kept looking around, waiting, almost expecting something to jump out at him. Whether it was just a sign of something to come, or an actual person, he was waiting for a surprise. But as he got to the door, it still hadn't come. He opened the door, letting Gunner go through first. As he walked in, he had his hand behind his back, ready to withdraw the gun out of the belt of his pants. He saw the same person sitting at the desk as the last time he was there. Once again, he got a warm and friendly greeting.

"Hi. Nice to see you again," the woman said.

Jacobs looked at her and tried to smile, though he was still feeling uneasy about being there. He quickly turned his head to both sides. "Is uh... is Eddie here?"

"Eddie? Yes, he is. You must be Brett."

Jacobs gave a slight nod. "Yeah."

"He said you'd be coming. Just go straight down the hall there to the right. He's in Deb's room."

Jacobs had an uncomfortable look about him as he looked down the hall. He thanked the woman and started to proceed. "Hope he's not... never mind. Just stop talking. Don't even think about it," he said to himself.

Once Jacobs got to the door, he put his ear up to it, trying to hear inside. He heard a couple of voices and what seemed to be laughs and giggles. If this was a setup, it'd be the strangest one he'd ever heard of. He took a look back at the door behind him which was also closed. He looked down at Gunner who had taken a seat.

"Here we go," Jacobs said.

He knocked on the door, though not very loudly. Part of him was hoping no one would answer so he could just go away. He had no such luck, however, as the door swung open only a few seconds later. Deb appeared in the doorway, only partially dressed. She had a thong on, but no top to cover her large breasts, and like the last time Jacobs saw her, she didn't seem to care.

"Is Eddie here?" Jacobs asked, trying to keep his eyes focused on her face.

"In here," Deb replied, backing up, and putting her arm out to welcome him in.

As Jacobs walked in, his eyes immediately noticed

movement to his right. As he looked over there, he saw Franks' naked body getting up off the couch.

"Awe, man, what are you doing?" Jacobs angrily asked, knowing he wasn't going to be able to shake that vision from his mind for quite a while. He turned away and looked at the wall, keeping his back to Franks.

"Oh, hey, I see you found me," Franks said, standing up and putting his pants on.

"Yeah, well, I was hoping not to find so much of you."

Franks laughed. "Ha. I see what you did there."

"And I see what you did there," Jacobs said, still looking at the wall.

"Got here quicker than I thought. Didn't expect you for a few more minutes," Franks said, still getting dressed.

"Lucky me. I got here early."

Deb came over to Jacobs and put one hand on his back, rubbing it, while she had a drink in the other hand. "Want one?"

"No thanks, but I'd settle for some burning sticks so I can poke my eyes out."

Deb laughed, then went over to the couch and sat down. "It's safe to look now."

Hoping he wasn't being toyed with, Jacobs slowly turned around, though he had his eyes closed, almost afraid to look and find out. He slowly opened one eye and found that Franks was indeed dressed fully by now.

"You mind telling me what I'm doing here and why you wanted me to see your naked ass?" Jacobs asked.

"Oh, well, you see it goes like this, it's not about me."

"Could've fooled me."

"Well, I mean, I didn't bring you here to see me."

"Eddie, you better get to the point quickly or else I'm gonna beat you to death right here."

"Oh, OK, I can see you're not in a great mood for some reason."

"Eddie!"

"OK. Well, it's about Lucy."

"What about her?" Jacobs asked.

Franks looked at Deb first and nodded. She got up and left the room, walking across the hallway. Jacobs watched her leave, then turned his attention back to Franks.

"Eddie, I'm not really in the mood for games. You cryptically got me here under very vague circumstances, then I walk in and see your naked tush, and unless you want me to go all bat-shit on you, you better start talking."

Now Franks had the uncomfortable look on his face, not quite knowing how to start. "Remember how I was talking to you earlier about helping people who might need it? People who couldn't help themselves?"

"Yeah," Jacobs replied in a terse manner, close to having the limit of his patience reached.

"Well..." Franks was interrupted as Deb came into

the room, her arm around Lucy. "Well, it's probably better to show you than to keep spitting out words."

"Show me what?"

Lucy stood there, almost looking timid. She didn't want to be there and told them both that she just wanted the whole thing to go away. As Deb pulled back the hair from the side of Lucy's face, Jacobs could see right away the nasty-looking bruises on her cheek to go along with her puffy eye.

"What happened?" Jacobs asked. His annoyance over being called there under questionable circum- stances was beginning to fade away. He was genuinely concerned over Lucy's well-being. Considering she was nice to him before and helped him when he really needed it, Jacobs was eager to find out her problem.

"It's nothing," Lucy replied. "I just fell. They wanna make a big deal over it."

"You did not just fall," Deb said. "It was that crumb, Jeremy Florian."

"Who's he?" Jacobs asked.

"Deb, just let it go," Lucy said.

"I will not just let it go. He roughed you over but good. And it's not the first time either. You keep letting him get away with it now, and he'll keep doing it until one time he knocks you down and you don't get up. I'll put up with a lot of nonsense from men, but physical abuse is something I don't tolerate from nobody."

"So, who is this guy?" Jacobs asked.

Lucy shrugged, still not wanting to get into it. Deb

didn't have any problem speaking for her. "He's a guy who comes in here from time to time. And someone Lucy sometimes meets outside of here, though I keep telling her to stop doing that. There are too many weirdos out there and you're put in compromising situations you can't control."

Lucy started crying, getting a hug from Deb as she did. After a minute of consoling her, Deb led her over to the couch where she tried to calm her down. As they did, Jacobs pulled Franks to the side.

"What exactly am I doing here?" Jacobs asked, keeping his voice down so the ladies couldn't hear him.

"I wanted you to look at her face."

Jacobs took a quick peek at Lucy. "OK. I see it. So what do you want me to do?"

"I dunno. Like we were talking about earlier. Helping people."

"Yeah, you keep saying that, but I don't understand what you want me to do."

"I dunno, take care of the guy or something."

"What exactly do you want me to do, kill him?" Jacobs asked, still keeping his voice low.

Franks shrugged. "There must be something you can do."

"Why me?"

"Beause you seem to be good at this sort of thing. And Lucy's a nice girl. You said so yourself."

"Yeah, she is nice, and I'm sorry this happened to her, but I don't know why you're involving me. There's nothing I can do. If you want my advice, call the police and tell them what happened so they can pick this guy up."

"And what's she gonna tell them?" Franks asked. "That she works in a massage parlor that dishes out a little sex on the side? They'll close this place down in a week."

"Yeah, well, maybe that's not such a bad thing."

Franks' eyes almost bulged out of their sockets, looking like he might revolt at the thought of the business not being there. "Aghast at your devious words. Bite your tongue at such an unpleasant thought."

"It'd be for their own safety. Then maybe things like this wouldn't happen."

"Hey, we both know there's people out there on street corners and hotels who do this all the time."

"Yeah, and they get caught up in the same situations," Jacobs said.

"So instead of having them out there on the street with some undesirables, isn't it better to stay here, under the same roof? Where you have a certain amount of control over things?"

"Except that she doesn't do that. You heard it yourself that she's gone out with this bozo. And I know it's not the first time she's done it. She did it with Mallette's crew too."

"I think this is what she needs to finally drive the point home," Franks said, really hoping Jacobs would change his tune.

Jacobs sighed, hating that Franks was getting him in the middle of it. Though he did like Lucy, he didn't really want to be fighting her battles for her. Or anyone for that matter.

"Please. As a personal favor to me," Franks said, continuing to plead his case.

Jacobs looked away for a second and shook his head. When he brought his head back around, he noticed Gunner had moved away from him and was sitting by the couch in front of the two women. They were both petting him, even getting a smile out of Lucy.

"See, even he knows a good thing when he sees it," Franks said.

"Traitor," Jacobs replied.

Franks laughed, though it was more out of nervousness, hoping that his friend wouldn't turn him down. Jacobs' defenses were starting to break down, but before they were completely shattered, he turned the questions around.

"So let me ask you something."

"Shoot," Franks said. "Well, I mean, not literally."

"So if you're all fired up about this new attitude of yours and helping everyone under the sun, then why don't you do it?"

"Do what?"

"Why don't you help her?"

Franks looked at Lucy, then back at Jacobs. "Who? Me?"

"Yeah. You."

"You know I'm a lover, not a fighter."

"Convenient excuse."

"Well, first of all, I'm not in the violence game. That's your bag. I'm in the information business," Franks said, putting his hands in the air and pretending to pick things out of it. "Little bits of information that I just pick from the sky and pass them along to other interested parties."

"For a price."

"Of course. So that's my thing. But roughing people up, no, I wouldn't do too good with that."

"So you want me to do it?"

"Well, you just took out fifteen of Mallette's men. What's a few more? And besides, it's not helping everyone under the sun, just a few that I know. And these people are friends of ours."

"You mean friends of yours," Jacob said.

"Come on, man, help a brother out. What else you got going on right now?"

Jacobs closed his eyes and let out a deep sigh, knowing he was about to be roped in. Maybe it was his police background, or maybe it was just his personality to not turn away somebody who was in trouble, but either way, he couldn't just turn away from Lucy and pretend that he didn't see it. He would never forgive himself if he walked away from this and he heard in a week or two that something had happened to her. Something that he could have possibly prevented.

"I know I'm gonna regret this," Jacobs said.

Franks smiled and clapped his hands. "That mean you're in?"

"It's up to her."

"She'll come around."

"And one more thing."

"What's that?"

"I'm not looking to kill anybody else," Jacobs said. "What's happened with Mallette... that's personal. I don't wanna kill everyone I come into contact with."

"Understood. But, uh, how you gonna get this guy to see the light if you don't flash it in front of him with his life in danger?"

"Sometimes people just need a good stern talking to to see the error of their ways."

"Well, I guess you're the boss."

With them in agreement, Jacobs and Franks walked over to the couch where the ladies were still petting Gunner.

"This little guy yours?" Lucy asked, her mood picking up.

"I'm beginning to think I'm his," Jacobs replied, getting a laugh from the room.

"Seems like he's got real good manners for a puppy."

"I've been working with him a lot."

"Go ahead and tell him about that creep," Deb said.

Lucy still hesitated, not wanting to get anyone else involved. "I'm sorry, I don't know why they brought you here. I told them not to. It's my problem, not yours."

Jacobs got down on one knee and grabbed her hand. "Listen, you helped me when you didn't have to. I didn't forget that. No woman deserves to be beaten. Especially one as nice and pretty as you."

He finally got a smile out of her. "I just don't want any more trouble," she said.

"Let me deal with it and you won't."

"What are you going to do?"

Jacobs shook his head, looking somewhat perplexed. "Be damned if I know."

"I just don't want to get caught up with people being hurt or killed because of me."

Jacobs nodded, understanding her point of view. "No good person wants to see pain inflicted on others. But sometimes that's just how life is. Let me talk to this guy and see how he responds. If he happens to get hurt after that, I promise you it won't be your fault."

Lucy looked at Deb, who nodded, hoping she'd let them help her. After a few more minutes, Lucy finally agreed. "OK."

"Tell me what happened."

Though it was a little uncomfortable for her to do so, Lucy retold the exact details that led up to the beating she received at Florian's hands. Once she was finished she started crying again. Deb put her head into her shoulder to comfort her.

"So where can I find this guy?" Jacobs asked.

"I have his address written down in my book," Lucy said, picking her head out from her friend's shoulder.

"I'll need it."

Lucy and Deb left the room and went across the hall to get the appointment book. As Jacobs watched them leave the room, Franks stepped up beside him.

"So, what do you think you're gonna do?" Franks asked.

"Like I told her, damned if I know."

"Oh. Good strategy."

"Guess I'll just go pay this guy a visit and lay it on the line."

"Oh. Well, I hope you know what you're doing."

"You have a better idea?" Jacobs asked.

"No, not really. I was just hoping that there'd be some fists flying."

"Don't worry. By the end of our conversation, I'm sure there will be."

## 3

_____

Wiggins sat at the table, wondering what type of mood his boss was going to be in. Even looking at him, he never could quite tell what the tone of the conversation would be. Mallette usually had some kind of scowl on his face even when he was in a good mood.

As Mallette was being brought in, Wiggins was nervous. He wasn't nervous about seeing Mallette, but he always grew anxious in the minutes before meeting him, wondering what he was going to be asked to do. It seemed as though the more time had passed, the more illegal, dirty, and immoral things Wiggins was asked to do. It wasn't what he signed up for. When he agreed to be Mallette's counsel over ten years ago, it wasn't with the expectation he was going to be involved in the day-to-day activities of the organization. He simply wanted to represent him in legal matters, for both the money and notoriety. Over the past ten years, things hadn't gone quite the way he had expected. And as much as he really didn't enjoy passing down information from Mallette to his other cronies, Wiggins knew he couldn't back out of the deal now. He knew too much. Too many things had happened for him to just walk away freely.

As Mallette walked to the table, he still had a little hop in his step. He was still a confident man. Prison life hadn't beaten him down yet. Concentrating on his various businesses that were still up and running was the main thing that was keeping him going. That, and figuring out how to deal with Jacobs. He hadn't forgotten about him. And he had no desire to let up on the pressure on him either. Even though there seemed to be a temporary truce between the two parties over the past few weeks, Mallette had no intention of letting that continue. He wanted Jacobs gone and out of the way. As long as he was alive, he was going to be a thorn in Mallette's side. And the last thing he wanted was to see Jacobs' face the day he got out of prison. He wanted Jacobs to be nothing but a memory by then.

"You know, every time we meet here now, I half expect to see his face," Mallette said as he sat down.

"I'm sorry about that. It wasn't my fault."

"It happens. I'm actually glad he and I had that little chat."

"You are?"

"It reinforced my position and my beliefs."

"Which are?"

"That I want him dead," Mallette said, anger in his voice. "Now."

Wiggins was perplexed seeing as how there'd been peace between them for a few weeks. He knew riling up trouble to go after Jacobs would only bring on worse things than had already happened.

"But... everything's been good the last little while. Why change that now?"

"Because those were his terms," Mallette replied. "Nobody dictates terms to me. I say what will happen, not him."

"With all due respect, he has the upper hand here."

Mallette looked at his lawyer with contempt. "You're a fool. This is part of the reason he's had the success that he has. You have no conviction. We will dictate life to him, not the other way around."

"And just how do you plan to do that?" Wiggins asked. "He's beaten us at every turn. You've tried to get people out, it didn't work. You tried using our own people, they failed. You tried bringing in someone from out of state, he didn't do the job. He's beaten us."

Mallette seethed, looking like fire was about to erupt from his head. "That's why you've failed."

"I've done everything you've asked me to do."

Mallette was silent for a minute, letting some of his anger dissipate. "Hanson was not as good as advertised. I expected more from him."

"I think he did as well under the circumstances. It was obvious he was set up."

Mallette slammed his fist down on the table. "He was supposed to be the one who was doing the setup." He then looked around at the guards, making sure he calmed himself before one of them came over and helped him along with it.

"Jacobs still has friends in the police department," Wiggins said. "That's the only way they could've nabbed Hanson like that. He agreed to meet with him, then had the police nearby to engage in a shootout."

"But why was Hanson even doing that at all? I was paying him to kill him, not have a chat with him. I could've had anybody do that. I paid Hanson to be invisible. It was a stupid play. He should've drawn him out."

"He did that at the funeral."

"And then he missed." Mallette's anger was coming and going in waves. Every time he thought about the missed opportunities to get Jacobs, his temperature soared.

"Maybe it's best to just let Jacobs be for a while. Let the boys recruit more men. Get the strength in numbers back."

Mallette shook his head. "Too much time. We've still got enough men to do the job. And I want it finished. I never want to wonder again whether he's gonna be sitting down here across from me."

Wiggins sighed, not liking what he was hearing. He

thought his boss was showing his impatience. He slapped his hands on the table in frustration. "What would you want to do?"

Mallette looked around the room as he thought about it. "He's obviously getting help from people. That much is clear. Whether it's the police, whether it's contacts of ours, somebody, or multiple people, are keeping him off the radar. We need to draw him out."

"We tried that already. It didn't work so well."

"We need to do it better this time. And on a bigger scale. Make the stakes so big he's got no choice but to show himself."

"Exactly how are we going to do that? His father's already been killed."

"He's got other family members," Mallette said.

Wiggins shook his head, not believing in the plan. "No, that won't work. It's already been tried. He's not going to fall for that again. He'll show up at the funeral the next day, or when everybody's gone, or he'll have a disguise. He's not going to show his face again there. He's going to anticipate that. You'd just be bringing more heat on yourself with people figuring you ordered the hits."

Mallette, unhappy, turned his head and stared at the wall. He knew Wiggins was right. Trying the same thing twice was a fool's move. "There must be something."

"I say we do the smart thing and wait him out."

Mallette shook his head, determined to make

Jacobs pay now. After a few minutes, he thought he had it. "Children."

"What?" Wiggins asked, not understanding.

"Children. We lure him with children."

"What children?"

"His brother," Mallette answered. "His brother has children, doesn't he?"

"Umm, yeah, I think so. I still don't see how that plays into it."

"You said it yourself. Killing his family members hasn't worked. He's still been elusive. So, we'll change strategy."

"You're planning on murdering children?" Wiggins asked, not on board with the strategy if that's what was being implied. He cut a lot of corners and did some unethical things in his time, but hurting children was where he drew the line.

Seeing that he was losing his subordinate, Mallette quickly set the record straight. "No, the children will be fine. We won't hurt them. We won't hurt their parents either."

"So what is it that you're suggesting?"

"We just take them for a little ride for a day or two," Mallette said, almost making it sound like it was no big deal, as if they were taking them on a trip to the park or something. "Put them in comfortable surroundings, whatever they need."

"Just to be clear, you are suggesting that we kidnap these kids?"

"With the understanding that they are not to be harmed. That's how we lure Jacobs out."

Wiggins shook his head and sighed, not really liking the idea. He just didn't want to get kids involved. "And how is that going to bring Jacobs out?"

"We spread word through all of our contacts that the kids will be released unharmed if Jacobs surrenders himself to a place of our choosing."

"What's to stop him from just getting the police involved again?"

"We'll up the stakes," Mallette said.

"How?"

"Let him know the first sign of police involvement, the kids will be shot." A look of horror masked Wiggins' face that Mallette quickly tried to erase. "Relax. We won't actually shoot the kids. Don't worry about it. Jacobs wouldn't risk their life by bringing the police in."

"But what if he does?" Wiggins asked, still fearful of what would happen to the children.

"The instructions will be that the children are not to be harmed under any circumstances. If things get too hot, leave the kids behind."

"What about police protection?"

"What about it?" Mallette asked.

"Well, they did have someone on the brother after their father was killed just in case."

"I'm sure that's over with by now. Besides, they can't keep someone stationed there forever. If there's someone still on it, find out for how much longer."

"And if there is?"

"Then wait until they're done or an opportunity presents itself."

"And if there's not?"

"Then there's a full green light to put this thing into operation now."

As silence grew between the two. Mallette could read his lawyer's face and could see that he was troubled by something.

"What is it?" Mallette asked.

Wiggins hesitated before answering, knowing whatever fears he had would be shot down immediately. He knew Mallette had his mind made up and wasn't going to consider anything he had to say. "It's just... are you sure we're not waking up the hornet's nest here? I mean, things are quiet right now. Why not just keep it going?"

Mallette's face grew angrier as his jaw tightened and he clenched his teeth together. "I already told you. Because I don't bow down to the demands of my enemies. He's the reason I'm in here. And as long as I'm in here I'm going to continue to make his life a living hell. Every single minute of it."

Wiggins knew it was a battle he was going to lose and wasn't even worth continuing to fight. He just nodded and agreed, accepting his boss' wishes. "OK."

"Now stop being obstinate and get it done."

"And if it doesn't work?"

"Why wouldn't it work?"

"What if he doesn't care about his brother or his kids?" Wiggins asked, knowing full well that it didn't matter and that Jacobs would get himself involved. It was a last-ditch effort by the lawyer to try and change plans. It didn't work though.

"It'll work. You make it work. Jacobs is a family guy. Wife, kids, siblings, parents, he'll go for it. Plus, he's a cop. Helping people, especially kids... it's in his DNA. That's who he is. There's no chance that he wouldn't capitulate."

"But if he surrendered for the freedom of those kids, he's gotta know what would be in store for him after that," Wiggins said.

"You can count on it."

"And you think he'd give up his life for theirs?"

"Absolutely."

Wiggins had nothing left in his arsenal to try and change his boss' mind. He had no choice but to comply with the plot.

"I'll let you work out the details. Where, when, time. Whatever you do, just don't pick the warehouse," Mallette said. "We've lost too many men there already. Jacobs seems to already know the place too well."

"I'll uh... figure something out."

"Just make it happen and get it done."

## 4

---

J acobs had just walked up the five flights of stairs on his way to visit Jeremy Florian's apartment. He contemplated following Florian somewhere, like to his job or to a bar, but Jacobs thought this way was more effective. Nothing was more likely to shake someone up than an imposing stranger showing up at your doorstep and threatening you. He just hoped that it would work, though his assumption was that it wouldn't. Men like Florian usually didn't take well to threats and didn't often listen well or understand what was best for them. But Jacobs figured it was worth the try. Maybe Florian would surprise him with how he reacted.

Once Jacobs got to the apartment he was looking for, he loudly knocked on the door. He heard what sounded like the TV so he assumed that Florian was in. Unless he was one of those people who left the TV on for pets when he wasn't there. Though no one was coming to the door, Jacobs thought he detected movement in the room. It sounded like someone scurrying from one side to the other. Jacobs assumed he was getting the silent treatment, or Florian was trying to pretend like nobody was there.

Jacobs wasn't going to have any of that. He was determined to make contact with Florian one way or the other. Not giving up, Jacobs forcefully pounded on the door again several times. After a brief pause, he repeated the action, hoping Florian would get annoyed with the loud, obnoxious banging on his door. After another minute, his plan seemed to have worked. It sounded like someone was scurrying over to the door. Then Jacobs heard the jiggling handle of the door as if someone was about to open it. The door opened a sliver, part of a man's face showing through the crack.

"What do you want?" the man asked.

"Wanted to talk to you for a minute."

"Who are you?"

Jacobs shrugged, not wanting to divulge who he was. "Just a friend of a friend."

"Go away."

The man quickly shut the door, but Jacobs was able to get a long enough look at the man's face to recognize him as Florian from the pictures they were able to dig up of him. Jacobs wasn't to be deterred by the door slamming and went right back to banging on it. The door quickly opened up again, this time a little further than before.

"Listen, man, I don't know who you are, I don't wanna talk to you, and if you keep banging on my door and don't go away like I asked, you're gonna have a real problem on your hands in a minute. So beat it."

Florian took a step back and attempted to close the door again, though Jacobs stopped it by putting his foot in the way. Florian angrily looked at him.

"Better move it or lose it."

"Tough talk for a guy who beats up on women," Jacobs said.

"What'd you say?"

"I think you heard me."

"Yeah, I did. And I think if you know what's good for you, you'll beat it right now, or else I'm gonna do some beating on your face."

Jacobs wasn't intimidated. The man was about the same size as he was and Florian's background wasn't one that Jacobs worried about. Though Florian did have a criminal record and had been arrested several times, it was mostly minor stuff. Nothing that really alarmed Jacobs and made him think he had to be wary or especially cautious of him. Florian tried to close the door again, but this time Jacobs stopped it with his hands.

"Does the name Lucy ring a bell?" Jacobs asked. "Works at a massage place if that jogs your memory a bit. Maybe you took her out a few times. Some welts and bruises on her face. Any of that sound familiar?"

Florian suddenly had a concerned look on his face. "Who are you?"

"Told you... it's not important."

"So, Lucy told you I did all that? Huh?"

"Doesn't matter where the information came from," Jacobs said. "What matters is that you leave her alone from here on out. If I even hear someone breathe to me that you roughed her up again, then I'll be back. And I guarantee that I won't be back here in as good a mood as I am today."

Florian snickered. "Pretty tough talk there. I don't think you quite know who you're messing with."

"Oh, I'm pretty sure I do. This is the last warning you're gonna get. I suggest you heed it."

"Dude, get out of here," Florian said.

He then gave Jacobs a solid push in the chest, making him stumble back a few steps. Florian opened the door further and stood in the frame of it, puffing his chest out a bit like he thought he was clearly superior and tougher than his opponent. But Jacobs wasn't going to allow himself to get pushed around by the likes of a woman beater and lunged forward, giving Florian a shove himself. With neither man backing down, a wrestling match ensued as the two men started scuffling, eventually knocking each other to the ground inside the apartment. They traded a few stomach punches and kidney shots as they rolled around on the dirty carpet. After a few minutes of struggling, they both got to their knees, still trading punches as they knelt, though this time they were exchanging facial shots.

Jacobs was the first to go down after a thunderous shot from Florian's right hand. Florian got to his feet and stood over Jacobs to unleash some more punishment. He reached down to grab hold of Jacobs' face, but Jacobs tripped up Florian's legs, making the man go down himself. Jacobs quickly got up and delivered a powerful hook shot to Florian's cheek as the man stood up. With Florian a little wobbly, Jacobs moved in closer and alternated delivering blows with his left and right hands. With relative ease, Jacobs maneuvered from Florian's face to his stomach and back again. Florian stumbled back to the wall, trying to put his arms up in defense, though he wasn't mounting much of an offense at that point. The beating was starting to take its toll on him, and his arms were slow in reacting to block the incoming blows.

It was about ten minutes of conflict, though it seemed much longer, before Florian's body finally gave out on him, slumping down the wall until he hit the floor. Jacobs stood over the barely conscious man, cuts, bruises, and blood staining his knuckles as he stared down his fallen opponent. Jacobs took a few steps back, still high from the rush of the battle, though he was able to restrain himself from taking it any further and doing more damage.

"This is your only warning," Jacobs said, still slightly out of breath from all the activity. "Stay away from Lucy. Or I'll be back to finish this."

Jacobs turned around and walked out of the apartment. Part of him felt kind of sleazy about the beating like he was some kind of tough guy for hire or something. Even though Florian deserved what he got, Jacobs still couldn't help but feel a little sad that this is what his life had become. Instead of enforcing the law and going home at night to a wife and kids, he was now operating in the shadows.

Once Jacobs got in his car and started driving away, he called Franks to let him know what went down.

"Hey, how you doing?" Franks asked.

"Wonderful. Just had a little chat with our friend Florian."

"Oh. How'd that turn out?"

"He wasn't real thrilled to see me."

"Is anybody?"

"I guess not," Jacobs said. "Anyway, I think he got the message."

"How you figure that?"

"Because it'll take him a few days to get over the cuts and bruises. He'll have long enough to think about it."

"Think that'll do the trick?"

"I dunno. We'll see. In any case, just let Lucy know I've seen the guy and had it out with him."

"I'll do that," Franks said.

"Also, let her know to watch herself. Just in case he didn't understand the message. Some guys get worked over and wither away and some guys come back enraged and looking for more."

"I'll tell her to keep an eye out."

"All right. I guess I'll see you later unless you have a list of some other people I need to work over first?"

Franks laughed. "Nah, I think we're good for tonight. I don't want to overload you right now."

Jacobs went home for the rest of the night. Once he got there, he cleaned his hands off and showered. After getting dressed, he went into the living room and plopped down in a chair. He felt exhausted from his confrontation with Florian. He stayed that way for a long time, just staring at the wall. He was contemplating what he was doing with his life. Everything seemed so clear after the passing of Valerie and the kids. He knew what he had to do. And for a while that seemed to be working and what he needed. But after his father was killed, he knew as long as he kept waging his war against Mallette, that the rest of his family would be in danger as well. The police could only provide protection for so long. Eventually, they'd be in harm's way. But now, if he temporarily halted his fight against Mallette's Maulers, what else was he doing? Just waiting for someone to call him so he could beat up some low-life?

As he sat there and thought about all the decisions he'd made in the last couple of months, the one he

absolutely didn't regret was quitting the police department. He did what he felt he had to do and his
thoughts on that hadn't changed. The one thing he did
wish was that he had killed more of Mallette's gang
before they engaged in their temporary truce.

Eventually, Jacobs' thoughts turned to Franks and
how he told him that he needed a purpose. The more
Jacobs thought about it, the more he agreed with the
sentiment. He did need a purpose. He couldn't just sit
around his living room for the next ten years until
Mallette was released from prison. Jacobs needed
something to keep him going. He just didn't know
what that something was yet.

After spending a couple hours pondering where
his life was headed, Jacobs finally fell asleep in the
chair. When he woke up the following day, though he
did feel a little better, he still had many of the same
questions about what he was doing. He spent a few
hours training Gunner, continuing to think about what
path he should be traveling on. He didn't do much else
the rest of the day except hanging out with his dog and
thinking. That quickly came to a sudden change after
he'd eaten dinner. He'd just finished feeding Gunner
when his phone rang.

Jacobs walked over to it without much energy in his
step as he expected it to be Franks calling with some
nonsense that probably wouldn't make much sense to
him. When he looked at the caller ID and saw that it
was his brother, he automatically thought something

had happened. With their father's death fresh in his mind, Jacobs gave his brother his new phone number a few days after the funeral. He wanted to make sure that in case of emergency, whether it was Mallette's men or something else, that Terry could get in touch with him if he really needed to. But Jacobs wasn't prepared for what he was about to hear.

"Terry, everything OK?" Jacobs asked.

"No, everything's not all right. The kids are gone."

"What do you mean, the kids are gone?"

"They're gone. Somebody took them about an hour ago."

"Who?"

"I don't know. They left a note."

"What's it say?" Jacobs said.

Terry hesitated for a few seconds, trying to keep his composure. "Says to not call the police or they'll be killed."

"What do they want?"

"You."

"Me?"

"Yeah. Says they want you to exchange yourself for them."

"You at the house?" Jacobs asked.

"Yeah."

"I'll be right over."

Jacobs immediately got his stuff together and flew out the door. With his foot firmly pressed on the gas pedal, he got to his brother's house in only fifteen minutes. Terry had kept his eyes peeled out the window in anticipation of his brother's arrival. Once he saw his brother pull up to the house, Terry met him outside.

"How's Becky taking it?" Jacobs asked.

"About as well as you can expect. She's trying to calm herself down."

"You call the police?"

"No, not yet. It said not to or else they'd kill them," Terry said. "Honestly, we don't know what to do. Should we call them?"

"Let me see the note."

Terry reached into his pocket and removed it, handing it to his brother. Jacobs began reading it and knew who it was from.

*We have your children, If you want them back again in one piece, you will have your brother meet us at the building address listed on the back of this note. That is all we want. When Brett Jacobs meets us there, your children will be returned to you immediately. You have our word that they will not be touched or harmed unless our wishes are not fulfilled. This will be your only chance to get them back. If we see any police activity, SWAT, or anything else that doesn't seem right, we will not try again. Your children will then suffer the same fate as the children of your brother. Tonight. Ten o'clock.*

. . .

After Jacobs was finished reading it, he turned it over to see the address written on the back. He was familiar with it. Though he didn't know it, it was the same building that Hanson had used to beat the information out of Williams.

"What's going on?" Terry asked. "Why did they take my kids?"

"Because they want me. It's still Mallette."

"So why get me and the kids involved?"

"Because they're getting desperate. They don't know what else to do."

"We gotta get them back. What are we gonna do?"

"We're gonna do what the note says," Jacobs answered.

"Are you sure? I mean, maybe we should get the police involved."

"If you do that, and they spot them, they will put a bullet in each of your kids' heads. Is that what you want?"

"Of course not."

"I'll meet them."

"You know they'll kill you."

"They'll try."

"What's to stop them from killing my kids anyway after getting you?" Terry asked.

"Nothing, I guess. But don't worry, I'm not gonna let that happen. I'll bring them back safe and sound."

"Why is this happening?"

"Because I've made life difficult for them and they want me gone."

Terry sighed and shook his head, not believing this was happening.

"This is why I've tried to stay far away from everybody," Jacobs said. "As long as I'm alive, I'm a walking target. And so is everyone who's around me."

"Doesn't seem like that's working very well."

"I'm trying the best I can."

It wasn't much of a consolation to Terry. "Yeah."

"I'll get them back."

## 5

A fter leaving his brother's house, Jacobs went back to his house to pick up Gunner. As he did, he called Franks to let him know what was going on.

"Hey, can you close up shop a little early?" Jacobs asked.

"Is that really even a question? Why, what's up?"

"Mallette took my brother's kids."

"Oh, man."

"They left a note stating that if I showed up at some building of theirs, then the kids would be released unharmed."

"You know they're gonna kill you," Franks said.

"I guess that's the plan."

"What about the police?"

"Can't get them involved," Jacobs answered. "Note says if they see any police that they'll kill the kids immediately."

"How much time we got?"

"Not much. Time they gave was ten o'clock tonight."

"That's smart on their part," Franks said. "Trying not to give you a lot of time to prepare and come up with a counterplan."

"I gotta get them."

"All right, well, hurry up and get here and we'll try to come up with something. I'll close the store."

After Jacobs got Gunner, he started making his way to the pawn shop. About half way there he got another call. This time it was from Buchanan.

"Brett, what are you doing right now?"

Jacobs wondered if his brother called the police and told them about the kidnapping. "Umm, just running a few errands. Why?"

"Just wanted to give you a heads-up on something. I got word a little while ago that a bunch of Mallette's men were starting to move around like something was going on or they had a job."

"Oh. Well, thanks. I'll keep my eyes peeled."

"Have you heard about anything?" Buchanan asked.

"Uh, no, not really."

"Maybe it'll be a good idea to put some protection on your brother again for the next few days, just in case."

"No, I don't think that'll be necessary."

"Why not?"

"I dunno. Just don't want you to waste your time."

Buchanan thought that sounded weird coming from him. He'd have thought that Jacobs would have wanted as much protection on the rest of his family as was humanly possible. Declining it only started ringing the alarm bells for him.

"What's going on, Brett? Talk to me."

"I don't know what you mean. Nothing's going on."

"I don't believe it. Don't forget, I've known you a long time. Your father's been killed, your family's been killed, and here you are telling me your brother's family doesn't need protection. That's something I think you would jump at. Something's going on that you're trying hard not to tell me. What is it?"

"Really, nothing's going on."

"Then why wouldn't you want protection for your brother?"

"I, uh, just don't think it's necessary."

"Did you make some type of deal with Mallette?" Buchanan asked.

"A deal? No, of course not."

"OK, then. I think it'll be a good idea to put men on your brother's house."

Jacobs sighed, thinking everything was about to go down the toilet. If Mallette's men had people watching Terry's house, if they saw police sitting around nearby, it could blow the whole plan to smithereens. Who knows what would happen to the kids at that point. But he also couldn't have the police poking their nose around into everything, also putting the kids in jeopardy. At this point, Jacobs thought the best he could do was just lay it on the line with the sergeant and hope he could appeal to his senses and let him handle it without any police interference.

After what seemed like an extra-long silence, it only reaffirmed to Buchanan that something was going on. "Brett, talk to me."

"I can't really get into it. But trust me, you cannot put men on my brother's house."

"Just tell me why."

"I can't do that."

"Brett, trust me. Whatever's going on, maybe I can work with you on it, but if I get word from another source about what's going down, I'm gonna have to act on it. And it may not be in your best interest if I do."

After thinking on it some more, Jacobs decided to come clean and hope that his friend would see things his way. "OK, you're right, something is going down. Somebody's taken my brother's kids."

"When were they taken? I'll put men on it right away."

"You can't do that."

"Why not?"

"We already know where they are," Jacobs said.

"Great. I'll get a team together."

"No, you can't do that."

"Why not?"

"Because it has to be me. That's what they requested."

"Who requested?" Buchanan asked.

"The kids were taken a few hours ago. I'm not even sure how myself. I didn't ask. Must've been while they were walking home from school. Anyway, all that was left was a note."

"What'd it say?"

"That the kids would be unharmed if I met them at this place. Once I showed up, the kids would be released. It said if they spot any police then the kids would be killed."

"Jeez," Buchanan said, taking a deep breath. "If this is Mallette's men, they're likely gonna kill you."

"I know they're gonna try."

"And there's no guarantee they'll release the kids."

"What other options do I have?" Jacobs asked.

"Let me get a team in place and we can surround the building."

"And have the kids as hostages? What if they see one of your guys setting up?"

"We can do it real quiet. I think it's worth the gamble."

"I don't. I can't risk their lives. Not again."

"What do you mean, again?"

"Val and the kids died because of me. My father died because of me. I won't have three more kids die because of me. I won't take any unnecessary chances, even if that means I don't make it back."

"I understand what you're saying, Brett, but let's be honest. They're already there because of you."

"I know that. But I'm not gonna let them suffer the same fate. That can't and won't happen."

"Your mind seems made up."

"It is."

"I hope you know what you're doing," Buchanan said.

"Yeah. Me too."

"Well, if you change your mind and need anything, let me know."

"I'll do that."

Regardless of what he said, though, Jacobs had no intention of changing his mind. He meant what he said about trading his life for theirs. He wouldn't allow three more kids to lose their lives because of him. By the time he arrived at the pawn shop, it was already closed. Franks had the back door open waiting for him as he stood in the alleyway. When Jacobs got there, the two men, along with Gunner, rushed into the office to try and come up with a plan.

"I don't like it, man, I don't like it," Franks said. "There's no way you're gonna walk out of there alive, no way."

Jacobs let out a half-smile, not seemingly too worried about it. "It'll be a challenge for sure."

"They're probably gonna have twenty guys in there waiting for you."

"Could be."

"And yet you're still planning on going in there?"

"Have to. Got no choice."

"I think you need to bring the police in."

"Can't. They'll kill the kids for sure if they see police," Jacobs said.

"Let's be honest here, there's a good chance they're gonna kill them anyway."

"Maybe."

"Cut the crap, man, we both know who we're dealing with here. These are the same crumbs who cut to pieces your little ones. You really think they're gonna have a problem doing it again? They've already shown a willingness to do it. I'm sure they'll have no qualms about repeating it. You're not exactly dealing with reputable citizens here."

Jacobs put his hand on his forehead, then rubbed his face as he thought about it. Franks was right, of course, but he just didn't see a better way. It seemed no matter which way he chose, the kids' lives were in danger. He had to pick the lesser of two evils. As he sat there thinking, Franks felt the obligation to also point out what neither of them had said, though he hoped that it wasn't the case. Still, it needed to be said.

"There's also the possibility that they're dead already."

The statement returned a death stare from Jacobs, who never even thought it a possibility until now. Not that he believed Franks was wrong or that it was some outlandish statement, but more out of the realization that Jacobs would not let himself think it. He couldn't. He refused to think that three more kids could die because of his actions. Even though Franks was technically correct about the history of Mallette's Maulers, that they seemed to have no problem killing kids in the past, Jacobs couldn't allow himself to think they would do it again.

"They're not," Jacobs said.

Franks looked at him sympathetically, knowing how he must have felt. But he also felt the need to bring it up and analyze the possibilities. "Listen, I know you don't wanna think that it's true, and I hope to God that it's not, but you gotta at least entertain that chance, no matter how small it is, just the chance that they might be gone already. And if that's the case, again, hoping that it's not, but if it is, you gotta be able to see that you're walking in there to save people who can't be saved. And that, my friend, means you're as good as dead too."

An agonizing look spread over Jacobs' face as he tried to come up with the best solution. "So, what do I do? Nothing?"

"Bring the cops in, man. Bring them in, smoke these dudes out. That's the best option you got right now."

Jacobs closed his eyes and buried his head in his hands as he brooded over his options. He then started shaking his head. "I can't do it. I know everything you're saying is technically right, and you may be right about everything, but if there's even the slightest chance, the tiniest of possibilities that they're still alive, I have to go under that assumption. And if that means giving myself up for them then I have to take that chance."

"Even though it's a trap? Or that you might be trading yourself for nothing?"

"Even if that's the case."

"I dunno, man, you're putting a lot of faith into an organization that's proven to be as ruthless as they come."

"It's not faith. It's hope."

## 6

It was only a few minutes before the requested meeting time of ten o'clock. Jacobs, Franks, and Gunner were still sitting in the pawn shop owner's car a few blocks away from the building, as they had been for the past thirty minutes. They were still going over different plans and options, though they hadn't yet agreed on anything. Jacobs was truly planning on just winging it, much to Franks' dismay.

"You're gonna get yourself killed, man," Franks said.

"Quite possible."

"You better not leave me with this dog."

Jacobs looked at him and smiled. "I thought you two were getting along better these days."

Franks turned around and looked toward the backseat as he felt the death stare from the dog. "Yeah, well, still the same. I'd rather he go home with you at night."

As the car fell silent again, Jacobs reached into his bag on the floor and pulled out a few guns and made sure they were loaded. He then put them on different parts of his body as he started to get himself ready to go. He put one inside the front of his belt, one in the back, one strapped to his ankle, and one inside his coat jacket. Franks thought he was wasting his time though.

"You know you're not getting anywhere close enough where you're gonna be able to use any of them."

"Never know," Jacobs said. "Gotta be prepared."

"You're getting stopped right at the front door and you're getting frisked before you go anywhere."

"Maybe."

"And if you choose to shoot your way in, then they might just kill those kids, assuming they're still alive."

"I know. I still gotta be prepared."

"What do you want me to do?" Franks asked.

"Nothing. Just wait. Maybe say a prayer or two."

"Neither of which are likely happening, just to let you know. I'm not real good at doing either one. If I don't hear from you in like ten or twenty minutes, and I don't hear gunfire either, I'm sending the dog in."

Jacobs was about to argue against it but then thought better of it. Maybe it wouldn't be such a bad idea, though he did worry about Gunner getting hurt along with him. If this was the end for Jacobs, and he was going down, he really didn't want anyone else going down with him. But if the dog could help prevent that end, he knew he should probably utilize him the best he could.

"Are there any commands I should know or anything?" Franks asked.

"You bringing him in?"

"Hell, no. I'll just find a way to get him inside and then the rest is up to him. And you. You know I'll help you the best I can, but gunning it out with these guys ain't exactly my idea of a good time. And I have no plans on joining you in the hereafter... at least not right now."

"If you just get him in, I'll do the rest," Jacobs said.

"Works for me."

"Wish me luck."

Jacobs got out of the car and started walking for the building. He walked slow and tried to stay as close to the buildings as possible, just in case they had look-outs or snipers in place. Sniping from a distance wasn't really their style as they were more the up-close kind of killers, though it was always possible they brought in someone like they did with Hanson. Jacobs kept his eyes peeled for doors, windows, or any other openings in the buildings as he passed them. He walked a couple blocks without incident until he got within sight of the building in question.

Jacobs stood there, almost paralyzed as he analyzed the building. He waited a few minutes before moving, trying to find some sign of movement within it. As he waited, he pulled out his phone to call Franks. As the phone rang, Jacobs looked up at all the rooftops of the buildings surrounding him, almost hoping to see the barrel of a rifle sticking out somewhere along the edges.

"Hey, that was quick," Franks said.

"I didn't go in yet."

"Considering there's not a backload of gunfire in the background, I kind of figured. What are you doing?"

"Just staring at the building right now. Kind of sizing everything up," Jacobs said, looking at the nearby buildings again.

"How's it looking?"

"Quiet."

"Doesn't it always before the storm hits?"

"Yeah, I guess," Jacobs said, his voice trailing off. "I dunno. Something just seems off."

"How so?"

"Not sure. Can't put my finger on it. Just seems weird for some reason."

"There's trouble brewing for sure," Franks said. "Just waiting to rise up and strike."

"Maybe. I would've thought they'd have had somebody watching from high above."

"Maybe they don't figure they need to."

"Could be, I suppose."

"Maybe it's just your nerves."

"I'm not anxious," Jacobs said. "Just apprehensive."

"Well, put your phone away, but keep it on so I can hear what's going on."

"All right."

Jacobs did as Franks asked as he put his phone in his pocket. He took another look around, though he still didn't see anything nefarious. He took a few deep breaths as he readied himself to move from his current spot. He ran across the street until he hit the side of the office building, still somewhat expecting some gunfire to be launched in his direction. Jacobs spun his head around again, but saw nothing. He clung to the side of the building as he made his way around the side until he reached the front. Once he finally got within reach of the door, he stopped again, waiting for someone to come out and greet him. He was still under the assumption that he was being watched the whole time, though he had nothing to base that on. There was still no one within sight.

Jacobs could feel that something wasn't right. He didn't know what it was, but that nagging feeling kept tugging at him and wouldn't go away. He took his right hand and withdrew one of his guns out of the belt of his pants. With his free hand, he latched onto the handle of the door and yanked on it, surprised that it pulled open so easily. The unlocked door raised the hairs on the back of his neck, assuming that someone was inside waiting for him and were granting him easy access.

Thinking that he might catch a bullet as soon as he

walked through the door, Jacobs got down on his knees and scurried inside. He figured that if someone was planning on shooting at him, they'd likely be aiming higher. He scuffled along the floor, still keeping low and clinging to the wall as he aimed his gun in front of him, ready to fire. But there was nothing. Jacobs wasn't sure what was happening. There were no lights on and visibility in the darkened room was low. He quickly grabbed his flashlight and attached it to the barrel of his weapon. He scanned the room, his gun going from left to right, until he finally cleared it. Jacobs reached into his pocket and grabbed his phone, pinning it to his ear with his shoulder.

"There's nobody here," Jacobs whispered.

"You scan the whole place already?"

"Just the part inside the front door."

"You still got a long way to go," Franks said. "They might be trying to lull you into a false sense of security or something. Keep your guard up."

"Yeah. I left the front door open if you wanna send Gunner in."

"I'll bring him up."

"Just keep your own eyes open in case they got someone stashed out there and they take a shot at you."

"I'll be the mother of caution."

"All right. I'm gonna keep on going."

"How's the dog gonna find you?"

"Just let him in. He'll find me."

Jacobs saw steps to the right of him and slowly walked over to them. He stood at the base of them and looked up, shining his flashlight toward the top. He cautiously went up, ready for action at any given second. Once he got to the top, Jacobs quickly scanned his gun around and went in the first room he saw. After he cleared it, he went to another. He kept up the pattern until he was finally in the last one. As he was finishing up, he heard a sound coming from downstairs. The sound was quickly moving towards him and at a frenetic pace. Jacobs went to the edge of the door and remained out of sight as he investigated. Within a few seconds though, he could hear the panting of a dog. He knew it was Gunner. Less than a minute later, Gunner eagerly ran through the door, then wagged his tail profusely as he saw Jacobs and sat by his legs.

"Good boy," Jacobs said, petting his head. Jacobs got out of his phone again to talk to Franks. "Hey, Gunner found me."

"Good."

"You inside?"

"No, I'm just walking on the street, trying to look casual."

"All right."

Jacobs put the phone back in his pocket as he began his search through the rest of the building. He stepped back into the hallway, Gunner right behind him. "Gunner, heel," Jacobs said, getting the dog to walk next to him until he was directed to do otherwise.

The two of them descended the steps until they reached the bottom. Jacobs rechecked the area he came in at, plus a couple rooms that were situated directly off it. Gunner stayed by his side the entire time. As they reached a couple more rooms, Jacobs decided to put the dog's instincts to work and see how well his training was paying off.

"Gunner, seek."

It was Jacobs' command to have the dog find anyone else in the area. If he did, then Gunner would start barking. Gunner was doing exceptionally well in training, partly because he was an extremely intelligent dog, and partly because they spent several hours every day going over things. But this was one of the commands that Gunner was having some problems with at times. He was hit and miss at doing what Jacobs wanted. The only people Jacobs had at his disposal to help with the command in training was Franks and Hack. Sometimes Gunner would perform flawlessly and bark at the sight of them. But sometimes he'd go right up to them and look to be pet. Jacobs had to hope that Gunner would do what he wanted if he saw a stranger in there.

It only took a few seconds before Jacobs heard Gunner barking. It was quickly followed by the sound of a man's voice. It sounded more like a groan than actual words. Jacobs assumed that whoever was in there was taken by surprise at the sight of the dog. Jacobs, fearful of something happening to Gunner if he waited too long to enter, didn't waste any more time in finding out what Gunner was seeing. Again mindful of making himself a target, Jacobs crouched down as he entered the room, eventually dropping to a knee. The man in the room saw the outline of who he assumed to be Jacobs coming in and opened fire. The bullets flew over Jacobs' head and grazed the frame of the door.

With Gunner still barking, Jacobs immediately recognized where his voice was coming from and shone the beam from his flashlight directly onto the man who was waiting in the corner. Seeing the man pointing the gun at him, Jacobs aimed his gun at the man's chest and ripped three rounds right into him. The man instantly fell forward, landing on his stomach. Jacobs scanned the rest of the room, then went over to the man still lying on the floor. He wasn't moving, leading Jacobs to believe he was dead, but he still checked his pulse. The man didn't have one. With his work in the room dead, Jacobs went back to the door, ready to continue.

"Gunner, heel."

With Gunner back at his side again, the two began clearing the rest of the floor. As they did, Jacobs could hear Franks' voice booming over the phone that was still on in his pocket. With all the commotion, Jacobs had forgotten that it was still on.

"Brett! Brett!"

"Yeah?"

"You all right? I heard the shots."

"Yeah. I'm good," Jacobs replied. "But there's another guy in here who isn't."

"One of Mallette's bunch?"

"I dunno. I don't recognize him and I ain't got time to really check him out too good. I just know he's dead."

"What happened?"

"Was waiting for me in a room. Luckily all that training I had you do with Gunner paid off."

"Yeah, I heard him barking," Franks said. "I promise I'll never make fun of those silly training sessions again."

"Glad to hear it. If you don't mind, I still got some more of this place to check out. Probably shouldn't stand here gabbing."

"All right, all right, sue me for being concerned. Just keep the phone on so I can keep listening."

"Will do."

Jacobs put the phone away again and kept on with his search. After they cleared the last of the rooms, Jacobs backtracked to a door located in one of the hallways that they passed over. Before opening it, Jacobs took a few deep breaths. Once he opened it, it revealed stairs that he assumed went into a basement type area. If the kids were in the building, they had to be down there. And Jacobs figured there were probably a few people guarding them. But that also meant that if he went down there firing away, there was a chance one of the kids could get hit in the crossfire. Jacobs had to be careful how he approached the situation. He took a few deep breaths, then looked down at Gunner.

"Time to go to work again, bud. Seek."

Gunner immediately rushed down the steps. Jacobs kept a careful ear out as the dog reached the bottom. It shouldn't have been long before Gunner started barking. Even if it was just the kids down there, he'd bark at finding someone.

"Brett! Brett!"

Hearing Franks' voice sound frantic, Jacobs reached for his phone. "Yeah?"

"I'm just around the corner. Looks like you got two bogeys coming in the building now."

"Armed?"

"Can't tell for sure. Looks like they both got something in their hands. If I had to make a bet on it, I'd say it was a gun."

"Thanks."

As the time went by without a sound from Gunner, Jacobs was starting to think no one was down there. He assumed the dog would have found someone by now. But knowing there were two more people entering the building caused Jacobs to change his plans. He was going to try and surprise and ambush them instead of letting them take the initiative. Jacobs left his spot and started roaming through the hallway until he came to the front. He got there just in time to see the two armed men entering through the door. As soon as one of the men closed the door, Jacobs announced his presence. Though he assumed it was more of Mallette's men, part of him didn't want to make a mistake. What if it was one of Buchanan's men? What if the police found out what was going on and sent men in? That would explain why they weren't there waiting for him already. One thing was for sure, Jacobs didn't want to make a lethal and horrible mistake. If they were police officers who were checking the building, he didn't want to engage with them. But he knew there was one sure way of finding out.

"Police, freeze," Jacobs ordered, dropping to a knee in case the men started firing, hoping the bullets would fly over his head.

The men didn't reply and started to get into firing position. That was a sure giveaway that they weren't cops. If they were, they would have identified themselves. They wouldn't come up shooting on another cop. As the two men started firing, Jacobs already had the one man lined up and squeezed the trigger on his gun four times. As the man dropped to the ground, Jacobs quickly aimed his gun at the other man. He heard the whizzing sound of one of the bullets zooming past him as he fired his weapon. After a few more seconds, the second man also dropped to the ground, partly onto the body of his friend.

Jacobs kept his gun pointed at the pair for a few seconds, trying to catch his breath. He then looked toward the door, wondering if there were any more coming. He waited for a minute, then decided he could ease up on his position a little. He removed his phone to talk to Franks.

"Eddie, any more out there?"

"Negative. You're clear."

"All right. They're both down."

Jacobs then hurried back to the door that led to the basement. He took a quick look around, wondering where Gunner was. He figured the dog would have come back to him by now if he didn't find anything.

"Gunner!" Jacobs said, whispering loudly.

Almost immediately, he heard the sounds of the dog running back up the steps. Upon seeing his owner, the dog wagged his tail and stood next to him. Jacobs figured the coast was clear seeing as Gunner never barked, and he didn't have a mark on him. Jacobs figured he would have if he ran into someone who was trying to keep him at bay or beat him off. But he still had to go down there and check for himself.

Jacobs slowly walked down the steps, Gunner right behind him. Once he got to the bottom, he flashed his gun all over the room, trying to get his eyes on anyone who might be down there lurking. If someone was down there, maybe they hid from the dog once they saw him coming. Since Gunner was still in training and this was his first real assignment outside of Jacobs' controlled situations, he wasn't totally confident that the dog didn't miss something. Jacobs wouldn't expect him to be perfect and completely reliable yet.

After several minutes of nervously checking the room, Jacobs was positive that it was empty. Not more of Mallette's men, not the kids, nothing. A lot of thoughts were running through his mind and most of them weren't good. He wondered what the point of all this was. Why tell him the kids were there if they weren't? Was it just a test? Were they hoping to get lucky and pick him off? Or was Franks right, and the kids were already dead? Jacobs had too many questions and not enough answers. He was just about ready to head back upstairs and leave when a phone started ringing. He instinctively looked to the one in his pocket, even though it was an unfamiliar ring. After making sure that it wasn't his, he started looking around. He noticed a chair in the middle of the room with something sitting on it. It was a small black object. As Jacobs moved closer to it, he could see that it was a phone. As he stood there looking at it, the phone rang again. It appeared to be a text message ringer. Jacobs reached down and picked the phone up, turning it on as he brought it closer to him. There were three messages on it.

"Glad to see you made it," the first one read. "We'll be in touch," said the second one. "Keep the phone for your next instructions," the last one said.

Jacobs sighed and shook his head, knowing he was working in the dark, both figuratively and literally. With nothing else he could do there, he went back up the steps to the main part of the building. As he maneuvered his way through it, he remained on guard, just in case there were any more surprises waiting for him. Once he got to the front door, he wanted to make sure everything was on the up and up outside.

"Eddie, you still out there?"

"Safe and sound, brother."

"All right. I'm coming out."

"Waiting for you with arms wide open," Franks said.

"No other activity around you?"

"Not that I can see."

"Why don't you head to the car and get it started."

"Roger that. I'll bring it over."

Franks quickly raced back to the car. As he did, Jacobs debated whether they should go outside and run to the car or whether they should just stay put. He still worried about someone picking him off if he wandered outside again. But if he stayed inside until Franks pulled around with the car, he was concerned about someone getting a read on the car and tracking them down that way. In the end, Jacobs decided they were better off staying put. Franks would only be a few minutes and it was safer than roaming through the streets on foot. Besides, Franks usually had cars with fake or stolen license plates that weren't traceable. He also had to hope that nobody recognized Franks, though if someone was outside watching, there was a good possibility that they saw him by now anyway.

Either when he brought Gunner up to the door or while he was waiting outside.

Once Franks arrived with the car, Jacobs sprinted to it and opened the door for Gunner to get in. Once he was secure in the backseat, Jacobs hopped in the front as Franks put his foot on the gas pedal to get out of there in a hurry. Luckily, and somewhat surprisingly, there was nobody firing at him. As they drove through the streets, Jacobs held the new phone in his hand.

"What'd you see in there?" Franks asked.

"Not much."

"Kids weren't there?"

"No."

"Find anything?"

"Just dead bodies," Jacobs said.

"Any clues?"

Jacobs opened his fist and revealed the phone. "Just this."

"What's that?"

"Found it in the basement. Couple messages on it saying to wait for further instructions."

"Further instructions? What's going on here?"

"I don't know," Jacobs answered. "I can't quite figure it out. It's almost like they're not quite sure what they're doing. I mean, why try to kill me with just three men when you've got at least another ten or twenty?"

"Or why not just go through with the deal as it was presented?" Franks asked. "I mean, you went in on your own."

"Unless this was just a test."

"A test for what?"

"Just to make sure I was playing ball," Jacobs said. "Maybe they weren't sure I was really gonna come alone. Maybe they were worried about me bringing police in as backup or something."

"But if that's the case then why send three thugs in there to try and knock you off?"

Jacobs stared at the window as he thought of an answer. "I'm not sure. Maybe they were hoping in the event that I did come alone, that maybe these guys would get lucky and kill me without having to go through any of the other stuff."

"Yeah, could be."

"Or maybe they had eyes on me from outside to see how I'd handle it so they could be better prepared the next time."

"I can even take it a step further," Franks said. "What if they had cameras on in there to see how you'd proceed? Check on your tactics. If that's the case, they know about the dog and will be ready for him."

"I think you're doing a lot of supposing with that one."

"How come?"

"You're assuming one of them is smart enough to think of it," Jacobs said. "With Mallette in prison, I'm not sure any of them are. I think without his leadership they're a disjointed group. After he gives the initial order, they're kind of left on their own to plan things out, and if things don't quite go according to plan, things start to break down."

"Yeah, you might be right about that. What do you wanna do next?"

"Let's contact Hack and see if he can check out the number these messages came from. Maybe we can give them a surprise of our own."

## 7

J acobs and Franks immediately went back to the pawn shop to wait for Hack's arrival. Franks called the computer genius on the way and told him they had an emergency that they needed help with. Though Hack initially balked and said he had other plans, as soon as Franks told him about the kids' lives being in jeopardy, Hack relented and agreed to come down. Jacobs and Franks were in the office doing what they could without him.

"When'd he say he was getting here?" Jacobs asked.

"Said he just had to finish something up and he'd be right down. Probably about an hour or so."

"And we've been here what, about an hour?"

"About that," Franks said. "He should be here soon."

True to his word, Hack showed up about twenty

minutes later. After Franks let him in, he immediately went to the office and started setting up his equipment.

"Sorry I'm late, guys, had to finish something else I was working on," Hack said.

"No problem," Franks replied.

"Yeah, a buddy of mine had his information stolen, and I was in an online battle with the guy who hacked him."

Jacobs and Franks looked at each other in confusion. "You what?" Franks asked.

"Well, the guy I was working on behalf of had his information swiped through a sophisticated virus and I backdoored it to find out who it was."

"Did you?" Jacobs asked.

"Oh, you know it, man. It was a tough battle, but I figured out who the dude was."

"Battle?" Franks asked. "What'd you do, engage in a battle of PC Street Fighter or something?"

Hack laughed, knowing how out of touch they were. "No. I just found out who the guy was and it took me a while to hack into his system. Then as I was hacking into him, he must've got alerted and started trying to hack me back."

"Seems like a whole lot of hacking going on."

"Yeah, it was a real struggle. The dude obviously knew what he was doing and had some mad skills."

"But you bested him?" Jacobs asked.

Hack looked down, almost embarrassed. "Well, you know... I don't like to brag."

"Since when?" Franks said.

"Anyway, it was a back-and-forth contest, each of us trying to get the better of each other."

Jacobs and Franks looked at each other again, neither understanding what their friend was talking about. It sounded like it was way over their heads. All they really knew was he was doing some computer stuff. Anything else was way out of their league.

"Oh. I got it now. Makes sense," Franks said, giving Jacobs a shrug to indicate he still had no idea what Hack was talking about.

"Anyway, what's up?" Hack said, sitting down at his computer.

Jacobs walked over to him and put the phone down on the table. "Picked up this phone. It was left by the people who kidnapped my brother's children. They left messages saying they'd contact me again."

"And you're wondering if I can track them down by the number?"

"That's it."

"Well, I'll give it a shot."

"Thanks for coming down on short notice."

"Yeah, no sweat. As soon as Eddie told me about the kids, man, that was all she wrote," Hack said. "I knew I couldn't sit this one out."

Hack immediately picked up the phone and saw the number the messages came from and plugged it right in to his computer program. As he did his work, Jacobs and Franks slunk into some chairs on the opposite side of the desk as they patiently waited for him to hopefully pick something up. It was an agonizing time for Jacobs as he nervously waited for word from Hack. Jacobs fiddled with his hands, tapped his fingers on the desk, and tried not to stare at Hack as he hoped for a successful signal from him.

Jacobs tried not to pester Hack with questions while he was working, not wanting to slow him down. Instead, he resorted to trying to read his facial clues, hoping he could figure out how it was going by Hack's expressions. By doing that, Jacobs could only assume that it wasn't going well. Hack had a tendency to crinkle his nose or raise the one side of his cheek as he did something. Maybe it was nothing, maybe it was just a tic, maybe Hack didn't even know he was doing it. In any case, it gave Jacobs some concern.

It wasn't long before Hack finished and came back with an answer for them. It took him less than an hour to complete everything, but judging by the look on his face, Jacobs and Franks assumed he didn't have good news to report. Hack leaned back in his chair and sighed, putting his hands behind his head as he looked up at the ceiling for a second. He didn't have that confident look on his face that he usually had when he successfully did something.

"Bad news?" Franks said. Jacobs chose to be silent until he heard something.

Hack brought his hands in front of him again and leaned forward. "Yeah. Doesn't look like there's anything to be gotten from this," he said, sliding the phone over on the desk.

"Why not?" Jacobs asked, a slightly disappointing tone in his voice.

"Well, for one, it's a prepaid phone. As far as I can tell it was bought at a retail store a few days ago. From what I can gather, it was paid for in cash."

"They're actually working smart for a change," Franks said. "Not leaving a trail."

"Yeah, unfortunately."

"Can't get a trace on where it's located?" Jacobs asked.

Hack shook his head. "No. Just a general area of around the building you found it in."

"So, someone else was there in the area and texted you," Franks said.

"Most likely," Hack replied. "But it hasn't been used since then so it's tough to get a read on where it might be right now."

Jacobs stared straight ahead at the wall as he digested everything. "They might not even use it again."

"Quite possible."

"The next time they contact me might be from a completely different number."

"You might be right about that. If they remain as cautious from here as they were in getting the phone and going up to this point, it stands to reason that they might not use it again."

"Which means they probably know you got some way to trace things," Franks said.

"Well, after that trick we pulled with Wiggins' phone and having them meet us at the warehouse, we kind of figured they'd start getting wary to this type of stuff," Jacobs said.

"So, there's nothing else we can do?"

"Nah, it's a dead end, man," Hack answered. "There's just nothing else I can do with this. I can tell you where it came from, where it's been, and how it was acquired. But I can't tell you who's got it, where it is now, or where it might be going."

"It's all right," Jacobs said. "We'll just have to figure out another way."

"Wish I could help you more."

"It's fine. You've done all you could. Can't ask for more than that."

Hack started packing his stuff up as he readied to leave. "Well, if you need me for anything else, let me know and I'll be right over."

"Appreciate it."

After Franks let Hack out, he came back into the office where he saw Jacobs still sitting there, staring at the wall, deep in thought. He sat down across from him and put his feet up.

"So, what are you thinking about?"

"There's gotta be another way," Jacobs said. "There's gotta be something else we can do."

"Well, I can't think of it except just wait until they contact you again."

Jacobs sighed, not liking that he wasn't in control of the situation. "I don't like them having the kids for the whole night."

"Assuming that...," Franks said, stopping himself before he mentioned again about the possibility of the kids not being alive. He figured that was a topic that had been brought up enough times already, and in these circumstances, didn't have to be mentioned one more time.

"What?"

Franks just waved him off, not wanting to get into it again. "It's nothing. They'll be all right."

"I just wanted to get them back into their own beds tonight instead of being held against their will with a bunch of murderous strangers."

"I know, but there's nothing else you can do right now."

Jacobs was silent for a minute, trying to think of other options. "What if there is? There's one person who probably knows everything that's going on."

Franks scrunched his face together as he struggled to come up with an answer. "You talking about Mallette? If you're talking about him, man, then I think you're wasting your time. Ain't no way he's gonna talk to you about this. He won't even own up to it."

Jacobs shook his head. "I'm not talking about

Mallette. But there's someone else who knows everything that the big boss wants."

Franks took another minute to think. "Wiggins?"

Jacobs nodded. "That's it."

"I dunno, man, I think that's almost as big a waste of time."

"I don't think it is. He can be reasoned with. Or at the very least threatened or bribed," Jacobs said. "Just like I did when I went to see Mallette at the prison."

"I dunno. Showing up at his office again might be risky. Might have more people stationed around the building as guards in case you show up."

"Who said anything about showing up at his office?"

"Well, where else you gonna go?"

"He's got a house, right?"

"You're gonna visit him at his house?" Franks asked in surprise.

"Why not?"

"Oh, I dunno, a little something called breaking and entering."

"He never reported me before," Jacobs said. "He won't this time either."

"First time for everything."

"He won't report me."

"When you gonna go?"

"No time like the present, right?"

"Why don't you go home for a few hours? Get some sleep first."

Jacobs wasn't having any of that, though. "I'm fine. I don't need sleep right now."

"Brett, you're tired, it's been a long day, you've had a lot of things going on. You've already had one battle. Get some rest first."

"Maybe if the kids weren't involved," Jacobs said. "But I can't go home and sleep yet if I know there's something else I can do to get them back."

"What if he's got a few men at his house in case you decide to show up? Could be that they've already thought of all this."

"Don't matter. If more of Mallette's Maulers are there, then they'll be having more funeral arrangements to attend to."

By now, Franks knew when Jacobs had his mind made up on something. He also knew that when he did, it couldn't be changed. He was a man that once he committed to something, he wasn't likely to deviate from that course.

"So, how you gonna handle it once you get there?" Franks asked.

Jacobs shrugged. "I don't know. I figured something would come to me when I got there."

"Well, I guess let me know how it goes when you leave there. Assuming that you do."

Jacobs glared at him. "I think I'll be OK. I don't have much to fear from him."

"And you're still assuming he'll be there by himself and leave the door wide open for you."

They discussed things for a few more minutes before Jacobs left. He was in a hurry to get to Wiggins' place. It took him roughly twenty-five minutes to get to Wiggins' house from the pawn shop. Before parking, Jacobs drove by the house several times, hoping to see if there were any guards on the property. Much to his surprise, there were none. After making several trips back and forth, Jacobs eventually parked down the street. He sat in his car for about ten minutes, just watching his surroundings. Nothing jumped out at him so he got out of his car and made his way toward Wiggins' house, a fairly expensive place in the suburbs.

Jacobs could see a few lights still on but couldn't be sure if Wiggins was up or not. Could be that he left some lights on overnight. As he approached the house, he noticed a couple of the lights turn off. He could only assume that maybe Wiggins was going to bed. It was almost two in the morning. Once Jacobs got to Wiggins' property, he ran around to the back of the house to try and keep himself out of sight. There didn't appear to be any security or guards anywhere, though he did see a sign that the place was monitored by a security company. That meant that an alarm would go off somewhere once he entered the house.

As Jacobs stood by the back door, he thought about how he was getting in. He then saw a couple of trash cans, one that was metal, and got an idea. Jacobs saw a stick lying on the ground, then grabbed hold of the metal trash can and started banging away on it with the stick. He then pulled on the other can, knocking it over completely so the trash started spilling out of it. He looked up at a second-story window that he thought might have been the bedroom, hoping for a sign of Wiggins looking out. He didn't see anything, though.

Jacobs kept banging on the can for another minute, not letting up. Eventually, the second-floor window opened up and a man's voice was heard yelling from it. Jacobs immediately recognized it as Wiggins'.

"Be quiet down there!" Wiggins shouted.

Jacobs didn't let up, though, and kept banging on the can, making it seem like an animal had gotten into it. He was hoping that the noise would be enough to draw Wiggins down and make him open the door on his own. Then Jacobs wouldn't have to worry about the alarm.

"Get out of here you damn cats!" Wiggins yelled.

Wiggins mumbled a few other things, then angrily slammed his window shut as he stormed out of his bedroom and stomped down the stairs. Jacobs smiled as he kept up his banging, amused and happy that his plan seemed to be working. Only a minute later, the back porch light turned on and the door opened up. Wiggins instantly saw all the trash on the ground.

"Awe, are you kidding me?" Wiggins said, surveying the ground littered with his trash. "I hate these damn animals."

"They're not too fond of you either," Jacobs replied.

Wiggins was barely able to get his head turned around before a right hand found its mark, landing flush on his forehead. Wiggins, not the violent sort to begin with, was caught by surprise and stumbled back, landing flat on his back. He opened his eyes again as he felt himself getting dragged along the ground. Jacobs had grabbed the lawyer by the collar of his shirt and dragged him back into the house. As Wiggins lay on the ground, Jacobs noticed a chair from the kitchen and brought it over. Wiggins seemed too stunned and frightened to move. With the chair in place, Jacobs picked Wiggins up and put him on in.

"Where are they?" Jacobs asked angrily.

"I don't...."

Jacobs knew what was coming out of the lawyer's mouth and didn't want to hear any of it. He wanted answers, not excuses, and not a runaround. Jacobs simply balled his fist up, reached back, and uncorked a powerful right hand across Wiggins' jaw. The force of the blow knocked Wiggins off the chair and onto the floor. Jacobs straddled over the fallen man and reached down to grab part of his shirt with both hands to bring him closer.

"Where are they?" Jacobs asked again.

"I don't know."

Jacobs let him go and delivered another shot across Wiggins' face. He knew Wiggins was in the loop. He was Mallette's mouthpiece to the rest of his men. There was no way he didn't know. Jacobs would beat the information out of him if he had to.

"I know you know," Jacobs said, delivering another punch.

"I don't know," Wiggins yelled, tears starting to form in the corners of his eyes, fearful about what he thought might happen to him from this encounter. A cut had also formed near his nose from the punches he'd already received.

"You know. I know you do." Jacobs forcefully manhandled the smaller Wiggins, picking his body up slightly off the floor only to push it back down again before nailing him with another shot to the face.

"I don't know, I don't know," Wiggins shouted. "I swear I don't know."

"Wrong answer!" Jacobs said, curling his fist up to hit him again.

"I swear I don't know!"

Jacobs didn't want to hear lies and let his fists do the talking, delivering blow after blow, hoping that Wiggins would eventually get tired of the pain.

"Where are they?" Jacobs asked, getting in Wiggins' face and shouting.

Wiggins started coughing up blood, looking like he was in bad shape. He was coughing, sweating profusely, and rolling around on the floor in a lot of pain. Jacobs was about to rain down with some more blows before Wiggins put his arms up, trying to stop any more punishment from being administered.

"Please... no more," Wiggins said.

Jacobs temporarily halted his fury, standing above the man with his fist cocked above his head, ready to bring it down. "Tell me where they are."

"I told him not to do it. I swear I did. I told him not to."

"I don't care about that. I wanna know where they are."

Wiggins twirled his head around, hoping he could somehow convince the man of his innocence. "I swear to you I don't know where they are."

"I know you had a hand in it. You always do."

Wiggins was breathing heavily and tried to catch his breath. "All I did was tell them what Mallette wanted. I distanced myself after that."

"Where are they?"

"I'm telling you the truth," Wiggins said. "I don't know. Don't you think I'd tell you if I did? I know you could kill me."

"You're lying."

Wiggins shook his head, at least the best he could considering all the pain he was feeling at the moment. "I'm not. I swear to you it's the truth."

Jacobs finally released his fist and stood up a little straighter, starting to believe that maybe the lawyer was telling the truth for once. He reached down again and grabbed Wiggins by his shirt, lifting him back up off the ground. Jacobs sat his prisoner on the chair again. Wiggins started hunching over as the pain was becoming unbearable. Jacobs wasn't letting him off that easy, though. He pushed Wiggins back, making him sit up straight.

"You don't know where they are?" Jacobs asked, his tone getting slightly less angry.

"I swear to you that I don't," Wiggins replied, his arms wrapped around his midsection, trying to hold off the pain.

"Then tell me what you do know."

Wiggins took a few deep breaths, hoping that he might just see himself out of his predicament. But he knew he couldn't say anything that wasn't true. Jacobs would see right through it. "When Mallette told me about taking those kids, I told him it was a bad idea. I told him you two had an understanding right now and everything was calm and to just leave you alone. But he didn't listen. He was insistent on doing what he wanted."

"So, you had no part in it? That's what you're trying to tell me?" Jacobs said, not quite believing him.

"Regardless of what you may think of me, I would never advocate or endorse harming children or getting them involved in this little war you two got going on. I'm not that far gone."

"So, you did nothing?"

"All I did was tell the others what their boss wanted. That's it. I didn't get involved other than that. I told them I wasn't handling anything, didn't want to know any details, wasn't getting involved. I told them to handle it however they saw fit."

"Then I guess you don't know where they're holding them?"

Wiggins shook his head the best he could despite the pain he was in. "I do not."

"What about what happened tonight?" Jacobs asked.

"Don't know anything about whatever you're talking about. Whatever happened tonight I wasn't a part of."

"A note was left with my brother telling me to meet these guys and they'd let the kids go. I got there and there were no kids."

"Don't know anything about it," Wiggins insisted.

"But there were three guys waiting for me who are obviously no longer around."

"Still don't know."

Little seeds of doubt were starting to creep into Jacobs' mind about Wiggins. He thought just maybe the man was telling the truth. He didn't seem to be wavering in his stance or flinching with his story. Jacobs continued quizzing him for a few more minutes, trying to get him to say something that would contradict his earlier statements, though he never did. Everything Jacobs asked Wiggins answered the exact same way he did before. He continued his steadfast denial about knowing anything that was going on outside of the initial order that was put out by Mallette.

Considering Wiggins wasn't a muscle guy and used to this type of punishment, Jacobs tended to believe his story. He didn't think that Wiggins would either be able to withstand the pain, or want to, just to maintain a false cover story. Jacobs pegged him as a guy who would roll in any which way depending on whatever benefited him most at the time. Figuring Wiggins didn't have much else to add, Jacobs was going to wrap things up and go home for a few hours to get a little sleep before starting early again in the morning. But he still had a few more questions he hoped Wiggins could help with.

"If I find out you're lying to me, I'll be back," Jacobs said. "And I promise you I won't be as pleasant as I am right now."

Wiggins shook his head. "I understand. I'm not lying."

"If you tell anyone I was here, your friends, police, bodyguards, Mallette, anyone... I'll still be back and I also guarantee that you won't be in as comfy a position as you are at this moment."

"Won't say a word," Wiggins said, realizing he was about to get let off the hook, though he also knew that his visitor meant every word coming out of his mouth.

"So, if you're not involved in any of this, who's calling the shots?"

"Umm, I don't know."

Jacobs wasn't pleased with the answer and looked

like he was about to resume the beating. Wiggins could see his displeasure and tried to hold him off.

"Wait, wait, wait," Wiggins said, looking like he was trying to think of an answer. "Umm, OK, probably the person who's leading things with this right now is... Johnny Wickers."

"Who's he?"

Wiggins shrugged. "Nobody special. Been with Mallette for a while now. Probably close to ten years. Loyal guy. Will do anything that's asked of him."

"Even hurting kids?"

"If that's what Mallette requires."

"How many men would he have with him?"

"Tough to say. Probably most of them. I would say at the minimum ten."

"So why the games? They tell me to be somewhere, I show up, and no one's there. Except for a few guys hoping to get in a lucky shot. What's that about?"

"Probably just what it was," Wiggins said. "Probably wanted to make sure you were going to follow up with your end of the deal. See what you would do. Probably left the other guys there hoping someone would get lucky or you'd let your guard down."

"So where would I find this guy?"

"Got me."

Jacobs gave him a menacing face.

"No, really," Wiggins said. "It's true. No idea where they'd be. They're probably not going anywhere that they've been before."

"Why?"

"Because everyone's getting weary of you. You show up at places not expected, places that they've done business in, gotten into their lives. They're trying to stay ahead of you. They think of you as a ghost now. Just randomly appearing in places and killing whoever's in your way. They're trying to be ready for you."

"It won't work," Jacobs said.

"That's their problem."

"I'll find them somehow."

"I don't doubt it."

Jacobs was about ready to leave and took a step toward the back door when he stopped. There was still another question burning a hole through his mind. And it was probably the most important one of all. One that he didn't want to think was possible, even though Franks kept trying to prepare him for it.

"One last thing," Jacobs said. "The kids."

"What about them?"

"Do you think they're still alive?"

Wiggins took a couple seconds to answer, not wanting to give the man false hope, or say something that would unleash his anger towards him any further. He needed to measure his words carefully.

"Honestly, I think they are. At least for now."

"For now?" Jacobs asked.

"They killed your kids without a second thought. You don't think they'd resort to doing the same thing again to someone else?"

"But that was different. Those were my kids."

"Doesn't matter," Wiggins said. "It'll still hurt you. It's still family. That's all Mallette cares about these days. Causing you pain. Making you hurt. Disrupting your life as much as possible. That's what he's about. He's willing to do anything to anybody if it means you'll get some sorrow out of it. He wants to drive you down so big a hole that you won't ever crawl back out of it."

"If they're still alive right now, how much time you think they have?"

"Probably a day, maybe two. They're not used to caring for kids. They're not going to keep them around that much longer. Your best bet is that they contact you again in the next twenty-four hours and that you can get to them first."

Jacobs didn't respond and simply gave a nod. Armed with all the information he needed, and that Wiggins had, he ducked out the back door to head for home. Though he hoped he could get a couple quick hours of sleep, he wasn't sure he actually would. Not with the kids on his mind. There were a lot of things going on that he wasn't sure of. But the one thing he was sure of was that he needed to find them soon.

## 8

_____

Jacobs' phone started going off at eight. He groggily opened his eyes and looked at the time. He was actually hoping to already be up for the day. He figured he must have slept through his alarm considering he set it for seven. So, it was a good thing that Franks was calling him or else he would have slept much longer than he was planning on.

"Yeah?"

"You just wake up?" Franks asked, taking note of Jacobs' sleepy sounding voice.

"Uh, yeah, it's fine though. I was actually hoping to be up an hour ago."

"Do you think before you do anything you can come down to the shop for a little bit?"

"Why? What's up?"

"Umm, there's just something I wanna show you."

"That sounds ominous," Jacobs said.

"Yeah, I would just rather you see it in person."

"See what?" Jacobs asked, getting nervous.

"Well, just come down."

"Right now?"

"If you could."

"I really wanted to start running that lead down that I texted you about last night."

"About Wickers, yeah, well, I'll get Hack down here," Franks said, hoping that would get Jacobs off his feet.

Jacobs sighed, not really wanting to get sidetracked with anything else considering everything that was going on, but he reluctantly agreed anyway. "All right, I'll be right down."

Jacobs didn't take much time to get ready, changing clothes and feeding Gunner. He was out of the house within fifteen minutes. By the time he got to the pawn shop, he arrived at the same time as Hack, who was just walking through the alley when Jacobs pulled in. They greeted each other, and as soon as they got to the back door, it swung open. Franks was eagerly waiting there for several minutes, continually checking to see if his visitors had arrived yet.

"Hey, thank you for coming," Franks said.

"So, what's this about?" Jacobs asked.

"I'll explain everything once you guys get settled."

Jacobs and Hack went in, going directly to the office where they were greeted by the sight of Lucy and Deb sitting there. It didn't take any further explanation for

Jacobs to figure out why he was there. He could see it. Lucy's face was littered with fresh cuts and bruises.

"Should I guess what happened?" Jacobs said.

Deb looked up at him and answered for her friend. "I guess he didn't get the message."

Jacobs glared at Franks as he walked into the room. He had a blank expression on his face as he sympathetically looked at the beaten woman. He looked back at Jacobs and moved his hands and fingers, without moving his arms, in such a way as to indicate he didn't know what else to do other than contact him. Though Jacobs was obviously saddened by what was happening to her, in the back of his mind he was thinking he really didn't have time for this. Not with three kids' lives hanging in the balance. But he also couldn't come right out and say it in front of anybody and risk sounding cold and callous. He also didn't have to say it as Franks was already reading his mind. He could see by reading Jacobs' body language that he wasn't totally into this and wanted to ease his fears.

"Listen, I know there's other things going on," Franks said, putting his hand out to relax him and prevent him from talking until he was finished. "I know, I know, that's why I got Hack here. I know you wanna start on Wickers, and that's fine, but I thought maybe you could deal with this thing first."

Franks nodded in Lucy's direction so he wouldn't have to say the words. He knew she already felt bad enough, and still wasn't in favor of getting Jacobs involved, and didn't want her to feel even worse by discussing her situation in anything but a positive light. He didn't want her to feel like she was burdening anyone. Jacobs stayed silent as he continued looking at the two women, thinking about his options. Franks kept at him though.

"No matter what, it's gonna take Hack some time to find the information we're looking for, right?"

Jacobs turned his head to look at him and sighed. "I guess so."

"So, what would we do until then? Just sit around here with our fingers up our nose? I mean, he's gonna need time to get the stuff we need, right?"

"I guess so."

"Well, until then, maybe you could, um, you know," Franks said, nodding at the battered woman again.

Deb looked up at him, hoping he would help. She knew he had a lot of other things going on, and though she didn't know exactly what it was, knew it sounded serious. She just hoped he could give a little of his time to their problem. Lucy continued looking down at the floor throughout the conversation, not wanting to make eye contact with Jacobs, or feel like she was being a nuisance. Before dealing with her problem though, Jacobs turned to Hack, who was sitting down and getting his computer ready.

"So'd Eddie tell you about what's going on?" Jacobs asked.

"Yeah, dude by the name of Johnny Wickers?" Hack answered. "One of Mallette's men?"

"Yeah. What do you think?"

"Well, I'll give it a shot. Really depends on how out in the open he's been, you know?"

"What do you mean?"

"Well, his digital footprint," Hack said. "You know, whether he's got social media accounts, I can get into phone records, public records, things like that. The more of that he's got out there, the easier it will be to track him down. The real trick starts when guys like him are basically ghosts and don't have any of that stuff. If he's good at staying under the bridge then it'll take more time."

"How long do you think? Just a general time frame."

"I'd say a couple hours at minimum."

Jacobs nodded, apparently satisfied at the answer. He then turned back to the two women sitting on the couch. He walked over to them and knelt in front of Lucy, making sure they were looking at each other face to face.

"So, what happened?" Jacobs asked. Lucy didn't answer and continued looking at the floor. Jacobs waited a minute for her to speak up, but she never did. After realizing she wasn't going to say anything, he tried to get her to relax. He put his hand on her knee and leaned forward, trying to get her to make eye contact with him. Eventually, she did, though she looked like she was embarrassed to be there.

"Hey," Jacobs said softly, maintaining eye contact. "What happened?"

"Umm, not much really," Lucy said with a shrug. "There was a knock on the door this morning."

"At your house?"

Lucy nodded. "I live in an apartment, but, yeah, basically."

"And it was him?"

"Yeah."

"What'd he say?" Jacobs asked.

"Not a lot. He was just really angry right away. He thought I sent you over to his apartment the other day."

"And he just started hitting you?"

"Well, I told him that I didn't, but he didn't believe it. He just forced his way inside and kept insisting that I did and that he wasn't happy about it. No matter what I said, he didn't wanna hear it."

Jacobs then pointed to her face where the new cuts and bruises were. "So, how'd that come about?"

"He just kept getting angrier by the minute. I told him I wanted him to go and not see him again. I think that's what finally set him off, me trying to get him to leave. He just punched me. Then while I was down, he grabbed my hair and pulled me around on the floor. Then he hit and punched me a few more times. I don't remember how many."

"Did you get away or...what made him stop?"

Lucy shrugged again. "I dunno. I guess he got tired. Before he left, while I was still on the ground, he kicked me," she said, pointing to the spot on her cheek. "Then he said if I tell anyone again, or if he sees you again, then he'd kill the both of us."

"That's what he said."

Lucy nodded, letting her gaze fall back to the floor. She started crying, causing Deb to grab her and let her cry into her shoulder. Jacobs stood up straight, continuing to look at them for a minute as he tried to process what she just told him. Though he initially was kind of disinterested, his mood was now changing. He was a little ticked off and wanted to immediately go find Jeremy Florian and bash his head in. Not only for beating up on Lucy, but also for thinking that he would, or could, kill either of them.

"So, what do you wanna do?" Franks asked.

Jacobs turned his head and stared at him for a few moments. "Let me know when you guys come up with anything."

Jacobs immediately turned around and walked out of the office. Franks started to follow him to see what he had on his mind, but stopped as he reached the back door. Jacobs took off in his car without saying another word. But even though Jacobs didn't spill what was going on in his mind, Franks knew. He'd seen that look before. Every time he went out to battle Mallette's crew, he had that same look on his face. It was a menacing scowl that indicated Jacobs was on the warpath and he was the wrong guy to mess with.

Once Franks locked the door again, he went back to the office. As soon as he entered, everyone looked at him. They were all eager to know what Jacobs was planning to do. Franks wasn't keen on talking about it either though. He just nodded to Hack to get him back on task, which was all the prodding that the computer genius needed. He could figure out what Jacobs had on his mind. But the girls didn't know him quite as well and were a little more curious.

"Where's he going?" Deb asked.

Franks tried to phrase it as delicately as possible without coming out directly and saying it. "He's going to try and address things."

Lucy took her head out of Deb's shoulder and wiped the tears off her face with her hand. "What does that mean exactly? What's he going to do?"

Franks looked around the room, still not wanting to say it. "I think he's going to make sure that he doesn't bother you again."

"How's he going to do that?"

"Well, he has his ways."

"Does that mean...?" Deb asked, getting the gist of it.

"It means he's going to take care of things," Franks said. "And it's probably best if you just leave it at that."

Lucy, also knowing what was being inferred, felt badly, thinking she was at fault. "I don't want anyone else getting hurt because of me. I don't want Brett to get in trouble because of me."

"He wouldn't do it if he didn't want to."

Jacobs drove right over to Florian's apartment. Jacobs wasn't sure if he would be there or not, or whether he went to his job after working Lucy over, but figured it was the best place to look first. If Florian wasn't there, Jacobs still had all the information about him from when he visited the man the first time. Luckily, Jacobs didn't have to go much further. He circled around the parking lot, making sure Florian's car was there before heading inside. Once Jacobs recognized it, he immediately pulled into a spot. Not wanting to make any rash decisions or jump into something without fully thinking it over, he made sure he was fully on board with what he was planning to do. He took a few deep breaths, then quickly exited his car.

As Jacobs walked up the steps to get to the fifth floor, there were no doubts in his mind what had to be done. Florian was a guy who obviously didn't get the message and wasn't the kind of person who would stop the deplorable behavior he was exhibiting. He pulled out his gun and made sure it was loaded before putting it back inside his coat. Once he got to the fifth floor, Jacobs stood near the entry way for a minute, contemplating his next move. The thought occurred to him that maybe Florian would be expecting him after the latest incident. Maybe he was even hoping that Jacobs would make an appearance. Given that possibility,

Jacobs knew he had to go in carefully. He couldn't just charge in like a bull in a china shop hoping to destroy everything in his path, because that path may have been booby trapped or littered with a deadly obstacle.

Jacobs knew he couldn't just stand there forever though, in case other people started wandering the halls. The last thing he needed was somebody to call the police and report him as a suspicious character walking around the facility. He moved forward until he got to Florian's door. He now had two choices. Either kick the door in and try and catch Florian by surprise, or knock and hope he answered the door. If he knocked, he'd have to make sure he stood beside it in case Florian answered with gunfire. There was also the possibility that he just wouldn't answer at all. If that happened, then he'd blow the surprise factor that he assumed he now had. If he knocked, and Florian didn't answer, and then Jacobs decided to kick the door in, there was a good chance that Florian would be in there waiting for him with a gun in his hands.

After thinking it over for a minute, Jacobs figured the best option was to try and take Florian by surprise. Not giving it another thought, Jacobs put his hand on the door to get a feel for how thick it was. Considering it was a regular apartment type of door and not too thick, he didn't think it would be too tough a chore for him. It wouldn't be the first one he ever had to kick in. He'd done it a few times when he was a detective, looking for suspects or trying to arrest someone who had a warrant out on him.

Jacobs put his ear against the door to see if he could hear what was going on inside. If he could hear where Florian was, or what he was doing, he'd get an idea of where to look once he busted inside. He couldn't hear anything, though. He then took a few steps back and took a quick look to both sides of him to make sure there were no curious eyes of neighbors looking at him. With nobody else in the hall, Jacobs lunged forward with a thunderous kick near the knob of the door, breaking it open.

Florian was sitting on the couch watching TV, directly in front of Jacobs as he broke in. Surprised by the intruder, Florian jumped up in shock at the sight of him. Knowing he was in for a fight, he hoped to get the upper hand by getting his gun off the kitchen counter. He rushed over for it but was intercepted by Jacobs, who ran towards him and speared him in the gut with his shoulder, knocking both men to the floor.

Jacobs wound up on top and immediately started throwing hay-makers. Florian tried covering his head with his arms to block the blows, but couldn't stop all of them, allowing a few punches to sneak through his defenses. They continued tussling on the ground for a few minutes, both men able to get in a few shots. Florian eventually was able to knock Jacobs off him and went on the offensive himself, though Jacobs did a much better job on the defensive side than he did.

Once Florian got the upper hand for a minute, he once again tried to make a move for his gun, though he was again stopped on his way there. As they wrestled with each other, they also started verbally assaulting each other as well.

"You're not tougher than me," Florian said, trying to get his intruder in a headlock.

"You're nothing unless you got a woman in front of you."

"Initially I was thinking about shooting you, but now, I think I might just snap your neck instead. It'll be so much more satisfying."

Jacobs kneed him in the kidney, breaking Florian's grasp of his head. "You couldn't take out anybody."

With Florian down on the ground, and Jacobs standing above him, the former detective looked over at the counter and thought about grabbing the gun himself and ending the coward's life. Florian tried getting up, resulting in Jacobs giving him a few more shots across the face to keep him down for another minute. Being too indecisive about what he wanted to do, and taking his eyes off his opponent for too long, Florian was able to regain himself and tripped Jacobs' legs. Since they were both on the ground again, they wrestled some more.

As they continued their skirmish, both realized that neither one of them seemed to be getting a clear upper hand at this point. They were both getting in their fair share of shots. After a few more minutes of rolling around, Jacobs knocked Florian over the couch. Jacobs walked around to unleash some more punishment. Florian tried to deliver some more of his own, but Jacobs blocked his feeble attempts. As they battled some more, Florian made an attacking move that Jacobs rebuffed. Wanting to finally put an end to the contest, Jacobs grabbed the back of Florian's neck with one of his hands, and took a firm grip on the back of his pants with the other one. With a good hold on him, Jacobs launched Florian's battered body through the sliding glass doors that led onto the balcony.

The glass completely shattered upon impact. A few bits of glass actually stuck in his face and arms. Jacobs stepped through the newly opened door and crushed pieces of glass underneath his shoes as he unsympathetically looked at the beaten man lying in front of him. Part of him just wanted to leave, hoping that Florian would finally get the message to stop beating up on women. But from his time on the force, he knew that men like Florian very rarely changed. They were who they were. And that was the part that scared him. Jacobs reached down and grabbed the top of Florian's hair, pulling him back to his feet. As Florian stood up again, though badly bruised, beaten, and bleeding, he still had enough energy to try one more blow. It wasn't a good attempt and Jacobs easily blocked it. To buy himself another minute or two, Jacobs punched him in the stomach, causing Florian to gasp for air and hunch over.

Jacobs sighed, not really wanting to do what he knew he'd probably have to. He closed his eyes for a second, then opened them and looked over the edge of the balcony down to the ground. It was a long drop from the fifth floor and Jacobs knew the man would never survive it. Jacobs felt guilty for a second, not liking what his life had become. But he quickly put that out of his mind, knowing there was nothing else he could do about it. It was what it was. Wanting to act quickly before he changed his mind, he grabbed Florian again by the back of the neck and launched him over the railing. Jacobs wiped his face with his hand, then looked down at the ground, seeing Florian's motionless body lying on the grass. He could see blood seeping out from the back of Florian's head. Jacobs knew he was dead. He took another deep sigh, but knew he couldn't stay there any longer. Police and onlookers would be there soon and make his escape a little more difficult.

Jacobs raced out of the apartment, stopping at the front door to make sure there was nobody lingering around in the hallway. With the coast clear, Jacobs left the apartment and rushed to the stairway and quickly went down the steps. He went out the side entrance and walked around the building to get to his car. From that vantage point he couldn't see Florian's body or if anyone had huddled around him yet. Jacobs got in his car, still looking around, paranoid about someone seeing him. But there was still no one on the horizon. He started driving out of the parking lot through the side entrance. On his way out, he could see Florian's dead body to his left. He slowed down slightly to see a developing crowd huddle around the dead man.

Jacobs saw all he wanted and needed to. There was no point in staying around any longer and looking at the carnage. He pulled out of the lot, still not a police car in sight, though he knew they must have been on the way by now. As he drove, he called Franks to let him know the outcome of the situation.

"Hey, how you making out?" Franks asked.

"Fine. Just wanted to let you know what happened. Is Lucy still there?"

Franks turned around and looked at her. "Uh, yeah, yeah, she and Deb are still here."

"Well, I guess you can let her know that Florian won't be a problem for her anymore," Jacobs said.

"Are you sure?"

"Yeah, pretty sure. He's dead."

"I'm, uh, well, I won't say I'm sorry to hear it, but what happened?"

"I'll spare you the details," Jacobs answered. "Let's just say he slipped off the balcony."

"Slipped?"

"That's what I said."

"Gotcha," Franks said, though he knew what actually happened.

"How's Hack making out? Any progress yet?"

"Uh, yeah, a little bit. It'll still take some more time though. But he's getting there."

"All right, let me know if he finds something out before I get back there."

"You going somewhere else?" Franks asked.

"Yeah, I'm just gonna stop at my place for a little bit and clean up first."

"You all right? You hurt?"

"No, nothing major," Jacobs said. "Just a cut or two on my face and hands. I'm fine."

"Good. Before I let you go, I guess I should say thanks."

"No need."

"No, there is. It was something you didn't have to do, something that was kind of forced on you, but you still handled it. Not everyone would have done what you did."

"You mean taking him out?"

"No, I mean just sticking your nose in it and getting involved," Franks said. "Some people wouldn't have done anything and said it's not my business."

"Yeah."

Franks could tell by the sound of Jacobs' voice that he didn't sound particularly proud of his actions. "Hey, I know it might not have been easy to do what you did, but this girl's alive, and will stay that way because of you. You should feel good about that."

"Hard to feel good about killing someone."

"Well, I guess that's what makes you you."

"How's that?"

"If you didn't, you'd be just as bad as they are."

"I guess."

"Don't guess. You're a good man. And that's not measured by the amount of lowlifes that you knock off. It's measured by the people you help."

After hanging up, Jacobs kept thinking about those words. Maybe they had some merit to them, but it was hard to feel good about someone losing their life, even if they weren't what was considered to be a good person. Especially when he knew Florian wouldn't be the last. With all the other things going on that Jacobs had on his agenda, there was likely to be a long line of people who would be joining him.

## 9

After stopping at his condo for about an hour, Jacobs then went back to the pawn shop. It was a little less crowded at this point as Lucy and Deb had left a few minutes earlier. He was greeted as usual by Franks, who looked him over for signs of wear from his contest.

"Don't look too bad," Franks said.

"I guess I've felt worse. Girls leave?"

"Yeah, they wanted to stick around and wait for you to thank you personally, but they had to get back."

Jacobs nodded, kind of glad that they weren't there anymore. Not that he would have been unhappy to see them, but he just didn't want to make a big deal about what happened. Truth be told, he'd rather not mention it again with anybody in hopes of forgetting it. Instead, he wanted to focus on what Hack was doing.

"How's it going, bud?" Jacobs asked, giving Hack a little tap on his shoulder.

Hack looked up at him and gave him a smile. "Uh, all right, I guess. Haven't really come up with anything worthwhile so far."

"Nothing?"

"Well, just the basics. You know, address and all that."

"And that doesn't lead us anywhere?"

"It does not," Hack answered. "From what I can tell, Wickers hasn't lived at that address for at least three months."

"No other way to trace him?"

Hack shook his head in frustration. "Not that I can see, no."

Hack rubbed his forehead, knowing how well that answer was probably being received. He was feeling the pressure too, knowing what was at stake. After sitting silently for a minute, thinking, something suddenly came to him.

"Wait a minute."

"You got something?" Jacobs asked.

"Maybe."

Hack didn't explain any further and just dug back into his laptop, typing away. Jacobs and Franks looked at each other, bewildered, neither having the faintest idea what was going on. They thought it was best not to disturb him and just let him go, hoping that he would soon explain what he was doing. After a couple minutes, Hack made a few groans, and a few whispers as he talked to himself, almost unaware that anyone else was still in the room. By that point, Jacobs' patience had worn thin and he needed to know what was going on.

"You wanna let the rest of us know what you're doing?" Jacobs asked.

Hack turned his head to look at him, and jumped a little, almost surprised that someone else was there. "Hmm? Oh, yeah, right. Anyway, so, what I was doing was..." he stopped, trying to think of the best way to phrase it without losing them in his technical jargon that he sometimes liked to spew out.

"Remember, English," Franks said.

"Yeah, yeah. So, I just suddenly thought of an alternative angle since nothing was coming up on Wickers."

"Which is?" Jacobs said.

"Well, I noticed that a name kept popping up as I searched for him."

"A name?"

"Yes. It came up repeatedly."

"So?" Franks asked, not seeing the connection. "I'm sure a lot of names popped up."

"Yes, but there was something different about this one."

"What?" Jacobs asked.

"It was a name I hadn't seen before. In all the work I've done for you guys, when it involves Mallette's Maulers, a lot of the same names regurgitate, right?"

"Yeah, they all work for him."

"Right, but one name popped up that had never popped up before so I made a notation of it."

"What was it?"

Hack looked down at his computer to make sure he had it right. "Addison Wickerson."

Jacobs scrunched his eyebrows together and looked at Franks. Something wasn't quite making sense to him. "Why does that seem familiar?"

Hack shook his head. "I dunno. But I've done some further digging and found something else interesting."

"Which is?"

"That's his brother."

"His brother?" Jacobs said, looking like he was taken aback.

"Wickerson... Wickers," Franks said. "Johnny shortened it."

"Why would he do that though?" Hack said.

"There's only two reasons why someone changes their name," Jacobs said. "They either get married... or they're trying to get away from their past."

"So, they're probably not close?" Franks asked.

"Maybe not," Hack said. "According to phone records, before Wickers went silent a few days ago, he contacted his brother about two weeks ago after not being in contact for what looks like a couple months."

"He was after something," Jacobs said.

"Maybe. They talked every day, sometimes several

times a day, for about ten days until it suddenly stopped four days ago."

"Strange," Franks said. "What do you suppose he wanted?"

"Sure wasn't just to say hi."

"I dunno," Jacobs said. "Maybe he was looking for help."

"With what?"

"The conversations stopped just before the kidnappings."

"You think Wickerson's involved?" Franks asked.

"Could be," Jacobs said before turning to Hack. "He got a record?"

"Pulling his info up now," Hack replied, looking at the details on the screen. He then shook his head. "No, looks like he's clean. Looks like he works for some manufacturing company. No criminal record. A few parking tickets, speeding, things like that, but even that, nothing in the last five years."

Jacobs sat down and started rubbing his head, trying to think of what was going on. "He the older brother? Younger brother?"

"Addison's the older brother," Hack answered.

"That mean anything to you?" Franks asked.

"I dunno. Maybe," Jacobs said. "I wonder if he could be talked some sense into."

"That's a lot of supposing without knowing much about the guy. You might walk right into it."

"I don't think so. Wickers changed his name. To me,

that indicates a guy who once he started his criminal ways, didn't want to remind himself of his original family name and what they stood for. So maybe he didn't want to be reminded that his family was actually on the up-and-up."

"Still a lot of supposing."

"Whoa," Hack suddenly blurted out. "No way."

Jacobs jumped out of his seat, thinking he found the golden nugget of information. "What?"

"Addison Wickerson rented out a building last week."

"For how long?"

"Doesn't say. Wait a minute, wait a minute, here it is," Hack said as he looked further down the screen. "Six months."

"What would he be renting out a building for?" Franks asked. "Unless he's starting his own business."

Hack shook his head. "I don't see any records indicating that. And it's not likely you'd rent out a building before you went through filing the new business forms."

Jacobs agreed. "No, you wouldn't."

"So, what would he rent it for?" Franks repeated.

"Maybe he wasn't renting it for himself."

"You mean he did it for his brother?"

"Maybe. Maybe that's what Wickers called for. To see if he'd help him out."

"But why?"

Jacobs thought about it for a minute before answering. "We've already seen them starting to change how they do things. More low key. More secretive. They're trying to stay away from buildings they've been associated with, staying off their normal phone lines, and using alternative methods."

"You're thinking that because of the other times you hit them, that they're using Wickerson to rent a building that they can use, thinking that you won't be able to find them."

Jacobs nodded. "That's what I think. Could be that's where they're holding the kids. They're thinking that if they use a name from someone who they know, but who's not associated with the gang, that it won't pop up on our radar."

"Smart thinking," Franks said.

"Yeah. But not smart enough."

"You think Addison knows what they're using him for?"

Jacobs shrugged and shook his head. "I don't know. It doesn't really matter at this point."

"You gonna talk to him first and see?"

"I don't see what difference it would make now. We already know where the building is. Only thing talking to him could do is tip off his brother. That's not a chance worth taking."

"Yeah, I guess you're right."

Jacobs then sat down next to Hack. "What kind of building is it?"

"Not much to it, really," Hack replied. "Looks like it

used to be a used antique shop. Not a big place. Got a first and second floor."

Hack pulled up some pictures of the building, both inside and out, from its former business. It had apparently closed down over a year ago without anyone ever taking it over until Wickerson signed the lease.

"Doesn't look like too many places to hide," Jacobs noted.

"Could mean it's not the place," Franks said. "Doesn't really seem like the type of place they'd keep the kids in, does it?"

"Could be why it's the perfect spot. 'Cause it doesn't seem like the type of place where it'd happen. Choose the opposite of what's likely."

"If that's the case then at least you won't have to worry about anyone hiding in there."

"I don't think that's what they had in mind anyway. I think they're planning on the shock and awe tactic."

"There's another question we gotta figure out," Franks said.

"Which is?"

"Whether they're staying there all the time or they're just using it for the exchange? Assuming there is one."

"One way to find out."

"Before you start playing the suped-up one-man army, how 'bout you take a step back and analyze things?"

"What do you mean?"

"Like, how you getting in there? It might not be as easy as some of the vacant places you've broken into. If they're staying there, like a bunch of them, say eight or ten, then you ain't getting in there by surprise."

Jacobs turned to Hack. "Was there a back door?"

"Uh, yeah, yeah, there is," Hack answered, pulling up a picture of it. All three men huddled close together as they looked at the pictures

"See, that's a solid door, no windows," Franks said. "Kinda like mine. You ain't getting in there by surprise."

"You could say the same thing about the front," Hack said. "If they are in fact set up there already full time, then they probably have one or two people by the door."

Jacobs sat there looking at the pictures, putting his hand over his mouth as he tried to think of a solution. After only a couple of minutes, he had two propositions.

"All right, tell me what you guys think of this. I got two ideas."

"Can't wait to hear it," Franks said sarcastically, though playfully.

"I can either get on the roof somehow or we create a diversion."

"What kind of diversion?"

"I dunno. A diversion. Somebody make some noise in back and I'll go in the front or vice versa."

"And you think that'll work?"

Jacobs shrugged. "Best I got right now."

"And the roof thing?"

"There must be some kind of roof access point."

"Bingo," Hack said, bringing up a picture of the roof and pointing to it. "Right there."

Franks shook his head, not really liking any option. Jacobs could tell he wasn't enthralled with the choices he presented.

"What?" Jacobs said.

"I dunno," Franks replied. "It just seems to me like none of these options are really workable."

"Why not?"

"Because there's no real possible way for you to get in without drawing a lot of attention to yourself. No matter which way you go, they're gonna see you way before you get there, and even if they don't, you're not getting in quietly. You're not getting in the back door unless you blow it open. The front's a glass door and they can see you coming. You're not taking them by surprise."

"And the roof?"

"Same thing, man. You're gonna have to blow it open."

"Then that's what I gotta do," Jacobs said.

"Hold it, Sherlock. Just keep your pants on for a second. There's some problems with that scenario."

"Which are?"

"First of all, you don't know where those kids are

being kept. If you use some C4 or something, you don't know how close they'd be to the explosion."

Jacobs looked disgusted and let his eyes drift to the floor, knowing that Franks was right and blowing a hole right through his plan.

"Second of all," Franks continued. "Explosives can be loud. It'll still alert them, not to mention everyone else in the neighborhood. You blow a hole in a door, cops are getting called immediately, and they might be on top of you before you're able to get back out of the building."

"There's gotta be something."

"I don't see what it is."

"I can't do nothing. That's one thing that's not an option," Jacobs said.

"How old are the kids again?"

"Eleven, eight, and six. Why?"

"Just wondering," Franks said. "Just thinking about how they're holding up through this."

"The eleven-year-old... she'll keep them together. She's a mature kid, acts older than her age. She'll keep them calm."

"Well, I agree about needing some type of diversion to get in there," Franks said. "I just don't know what that would be."

The three of them sat there for about twenty minutes throwing ideas around, none of which amounted to much. Then Jacobs thought of a wild idea. It was crazy, insane, and just about any other name one could think up to describe it. It also reeked of desperation. But at that point, it may have been all they had.

"What if I can get one of them to help?" Jacobs asked.

Both Franks and Hack looked at him with blank expressions on their faces. Franks shook his head violently as if he was trying to get something out of his hair. With his head tilted down, he whacked his ear with the palm of his hand like he had trouble hearing, even though he heard his friend perfectly.

"What was that?" Franks asked. "I didn't quite understand you."

"You heard me fine."

"You see, I didn't, 'cause I almost thought you said you were gonna ask one of them to help."

"I did."

Franks turned to Hack and shook his head, knowing Jacobs must have been going nuts. "That right there, that's just crazy talk. What do you mean, ask one of them for help? The only thing they're gonna help you with is an early grave. What's wrong with you?"

"You know, he might have something," Hack said.

Franks quickly whipped his head around. "What the hell have you been smoking?"

"Nah, listen, he might be right about that. Suppose you talk to Wickers brother? Tell him what's up. My money's on that he doesn't know what's going on."

"Oh yeah? I think you both done turned crazy. And

if you do tell him this, and he is working with them, boom, your chance of getting in that building turns to zero. You know why? Because as soon as he tells them you're coming, they fly the coop. Or they ambush you on the way in. You can't trust him. And you got no way of knowing if he can even help, or wants to for that matter, or get you in."

"Eddie, all you're giving me is negatives and telling me what I can't do," Jacobs said. "At some point, we gotta figure out something I can do. And we need to do it quick."

"All right, all right, let me think."

Before Franks had much of a chance to think of anything, Jacobs snapped his fingers in excitement. "I've got it."

Franks didn't believe him. In fact, the look on his face suggested he thought Jacobs was just waiting to say another stupid thing that he had to shoot down or throw water on. "Why don't I get a good feeling about this?"

"Wiggins," Jacobs said.

Franks looked at Hack as if he'd missed something. He was sure there must have been more to it than that. "You wanna say that again?"

"Wiggins. He can get me in."

"Dude, was somebody passing out drugs on the way in here or something? 'Cause I swear you're high."

"He can help."

"OK, let's just all take this down a notch," Franks

said, now positive that Jacobs had lost his mind. "Let's just take a deep breath, take a step back."

"I don't need to do any of that. Wiggins can help."

"You mean unknowingly?"

"No, I mean he can find a way to get me in," Jacobs answered.

Franks started blinking fast like he was having trouble processing everything. "See, that right there makes me think you've bumped your head too many times. You need to see a doctor and get your noggin examined 'cause I think you got a screw loose."

Jacobs shook his head. "Think about it. He's already cooperated with us several times. He looked the other way so I could visit Mallette in prison."

"Thanks to a threat."

"Nevertheless, still did it. Told us about Wickers."

"Thanks to getting beat up and afraid for his life."

"Still did it."

Franks rolled his eyes, still believing this might have been the craziest plan of all. "OK. Just humor me for a little. Suppose just suppose, that Wiggins is in fact willing to help. How exactly are you going to go about convincing him of this?"

"I'll tell him if he helps, I'll guarantee his safety."

"From Mallette?"

Jacobs shook his head again. "From me."

"And if...and this is a big if, if you somehow miraculously get him to help. Then what?"

"Then I bring the pain."

## 10

---

After initially bringing up his plan to have Wiggins help, Jacobs had to spend another half hour continuing to explain his position. No matter which way Jacobs spun it, Franks didn't think it could be pulled off. Not that Jacobs needed his permission or approval, but he did want him to be on board in case he needed him for some reason. After reciting his plans repeatedly, Jacobs finally decided to put them into action. The only thing he really needed Franks for now was possibly the getaway. Jacobs didn't want to be running away from the building, possibly under fire, and put them in further jeopardy. Once he extracted the kids from the building, he'd let Franks know, who would pull up to the rear of the building, ready to whisk them all away before the police got there. But all of that would only work if Jacobs could get Wiggins to join in.

That's what Jacobs' mission was for the next few hours. Get Wiggins' support. After leaving the pawn shop, Jacobs drove by Wiggins' house. He wasn't sure what the lawyer's schedule was, if he had to work, if he had a case, if he was doing Mallette's business, or whether he was at home or the office. Part of him thought that Wiggins might stay at home for the day after what Jacobs did to him not even twelve hours earlier. Jacobs thought that maybe his face might be too banged up to show it in the office. But once Jacobs drove by Wiggins' house several times, he realized that he wasn't at home. There were no cars in the driveway and no lights on.

The next logical spot to try was Wiggins' office. If he wasn't there, Jacobs would have to do some detective work. Either that or give him a call on the phone and hope he answered. Luckily, Jacobs wouldn't have to resort to such trickery or have to call on the skills from his former profession. As he drove through the parking garage attached to the building that Wiggins' law office was in, he saw the lawyer's car. Maybe he was tougher than Jacobs gave him credit for, showing up for work after being on the receiving end of several hard shots.

After parking, Jacobs spent about five minutes sitting in his car, thinking about how he was going to approach Wiggins with his offer. It wasn't going to be much of a conversation though. Jacobs was going to make sure he got his help. Or Wiggins would spend the rest of eternity lying next to his friends. If Jacobs had Wiggins pegged like he thought he did, he knew Wiggins would side with him. He was all about self-preservation above everything else.

Jacobs marched up to Wiggins' office and barged through the front door, meeting the same secretary from the last time he was there. She was quite alarmed at his presence as her eyes almost bulged out of her head once she saw him. She jumped out of her chair as he started walking past her desk to the main office.

"Uh, Mr. Wiggins is in conference," she said quickly.

"It's all right. I don't mind."

She maneuvered around the side of her desk as he cautiously approached the man, though she made sure she kept what she thought was a safe enough distance. "Uh, uh, excuse me, sir. You can't go in there."

Jacobs stopped to face her. "Why not?"

"Mr. Wiggins is not expecting you."

"We're old friends. He's expecting me."

Jacobs wasn't going to be detained any longer and stormed into Wiggins' office. The lawyer's face turned white as a ghost when he saw him, never believing he would be seeing Jacobs again so soon. Wiggins was on the phone, but stood up, letting the receiver drop out of his hand. It made a loud bang as it fell on the desk, snapping Wiggins out of his stare, remembering the conversation he was just having. He picked the phone up again and started talking.

"Uh, listen, Phil, something just came up. I'll, uh, I'll talk to you later."

Wiggins put the phone down as he looked at his secretary who was standing in the doorway. He then glanced at Jacobs who was now right in front of his desk.

"I'm sorry, Mr. Wiggins, I couldn't stop him from coming in," the secretary said.

"It's OK. I'll take care of this. You can go back to your desk. It's fine."

The secretary complied and closed the door as she went back to her desk. Jacobs was just pacing back and forth by Wiggins' desk until the two of them were alone. After the secretary left, Wiggins stood there, not moving anything except his eyes as he watched Jacobs pace, looking like a man who had a lot on his mind. Wiggins hoped it wouldn't evolve into a similar situation as the previous night in his home.

Wiggins finally sat back down, figuring he was safe for the moment. He assumed that he'd already be on the floor and bleeding if Jacobs was intending to assault him again. "So, what do I owe the pleasure of this visit?"

"You can skip the pleasantries."

"As you wish. I must say that I'm very surprised to see you again so soon. I was hoping that our encounter last night would be the last time I ever saw you."

A grin emerged on Jacobs' face. "Well, I guess this is your lucky day."

"What do you want?"

Jacobs looked around and pulled up a chair and sat down. "I want your help."

A smug look overtook Wiggins' face. "Well, that's an unusual but welcome change from our usual visits. At least you're not bashing me in the face already."

"If I were you, I wouldn't sit there and try to goad me into something that wouldn't take much effort for me to do," Jacobs said.

Though looking annoyed, Wiggins nodded, agreeing with the statement. The last thing he needed was to provoke his visitor into slugging him again. Though he only had a few small cuts and bruises that were barely noticeable, he was still really feeling the effects of Jacobs' punches from less than ten hours ago.

"So then, what are you here for?"

"Same thing as last night," Jacobs said. "Three kids are missing. I need to find them."

Wiggins sighed, not wanting to rehash the same conversation as the previous night. "I'll tell you the same thing I did before. I don't know anything about it. I'm not involved."

"And I believe that. I do."

"So, what are you doing here then?"

"Because I think you can help me."

Wiggins raised his eyebrows, surprised at the request. "In what way?"

"Well, I think I know where they are."

"Great. What do you want with me then?"

"Because getting in and out is going to be tricky," Jacobs answered.

"I'm still not seeing why you're here."

"Because I need you to get me in."

Wiggins looked stunned as he stared at his visitor. That was something he wasn't quite prepared to hear. "You need... me... to get you in? That's what you're telling me?"

"That's what I'm telling you."

Wiggins let out a laugh. "You're out of your mind. What makes you think I'm going to help you do anything?"

"You said it yourself last night," Jacobs said. "You told me you weren't interested in hurting children. That's what you said, wasn't it?"

"Yeah."

"Did you mean it?"

"Of course I did."

"Then prove it. No matter what side anybody is on in this little conflict between me and Mallette, nobody should be on the side of hurting children. I wouldn't do it to your kids or your brother's kids, or Mallette's kids, or anybody else. There are some things that should be off limits."

"And I already told you last night that I basically agree with that sentiment."

"Then prove it. Help get me in."

Wiggins sighed and looked away for a second, looking like a man who still didn't want to get involved.

"What is it that you want me to do?"

"As far as we can tell, they're holed up in a former antique shop."

"Mallette doesn't own any business like that," Wiggins said.

"I know. The deal to lease the place was brokered by Wickers' brother, Addison, last week."

"OK?"

"There's a steel door to the back of the place, and a roof hatch up top that I can't get in unless I blow them off," Jacobs explained. "There's a glass door to the front that they'll see me long before I get there. So, there's no good way for me to get in unnoticed unless someone helps me."

"And you want that person to be me?"

"You're the only person who'd be able to pull it off. Anybody else goes in there and they'll be suspected if they even get inside the place. But you...they'd let you in without a second thought. Especially if they thought you were bringing word from Mallette."

Wiggins didn't say a word at first. He just stared at Jacobs, not believing what he was hearing. "You're honestly sitting there asking me to turn on Mallette? You really want me to commit suicide for you?"

Jacobs shook his head. "It's not what I'm asking. I'm not looking for you to get hurt in this."

"But you are. You expect me to just waltz into this place, open up a door for you to slide in, then think there will be no repercussions for me? What do you think Mallette's going to do to me once he finds out that I've helped you?"

"Who's gonna tell him?"

"The ten or fifteen people who are inside that building."

"Can't talk if you're dead," Jacobs said.

"And what happens if one or two of them escape? Or in the event, no matter how small, that you wind up dead yourself? What happens then? How do I then explain it?"

"Then you tell them I threatened a member of your family. I forced you. Whatever you wanna say."

Wiggins laughed. "And you seriously think he'll care one way or another? He wouldn't care about that. All that matters to him is loyalty to him and carrying out his wishes."

Jacobs wasn't ready to admit defeat yet. He leaned forward, hoping something he'd say would resonate with the lawyer and change his attitude. "Listen, I don't know what your plans are or anything, but you need to do some soul searching."

"For what?"

"Because if you continue down this road, the day's gonna come when you're either trading places with Mallette, joining him, or settling down in your own plot in the cemetery. You're gonna need to start looking at your future and make some choices."

Wiggins intently looked at him without saying a word, just letting him continue with his speech.

"There's obviously two sides, mine and his. If you're on his, you can see what's been happening to the rest of his crew. One by one, they're all going down. If you choose to remain, I can't guarantee you won't be joining them. He's in there, I'm out here. You have a lot more to fear from me right now than you do from him."

Though reluctantly, Wiggins thought that Jacobs was making sense. "And what are you proposing?"

"Help me free these kids, keep them safe, get them back into the arms of their parents. You do that, and I'll guarantee you never have anything to fear from me again. You have my word on that. Unless you do something incredibly stupid."

Wiggins put his arm up to his face and covered his mouth with his hand as he thought about Jacobs' proposal. He couldn't deny there wasn't some appeal to it. Sensing that Wiggins might be swaying over to his side, Jacobs kept trying to convince him.

"If you've ever had the slightest thought, the tiniest idea of ever breaking free of Mallette and going back to being a real lawyer with real clients, helping justice be served, this might be your last and only chance," Jacobs said. "You and he are linked at the hip now. You know stuff about him, he knows stuff about you, you'll never be able to get away from all this unless you make the decision that that's what you want. But if you do nothing, search yourself deep inside... you know how this will end for you."

Wiggins rubbed his face as he was thinking of Jacobs' offer. After giving it some serious thought, he finally had a response. "I think I know how this will all end up for me no matter what I do."

Jacobs shook his head, not letting Wiggins give him no for an answer. "Doesn't have to be. There's still time. I'm taking out Mallette's men, with or without your help, and when I do, there'll be nowhere left for you to go. But if you start getting out now, escape from under his thumb, you've got time to rebuild. Make a new name for yourself. Go back to being honest like when you first started. I'm sure this can't be what you envisioned when you first graduated law school."

Wiggins looked away again and sighed, like he was deep in thought again. Jacobs thought he was finally getting through to him and breaking him down. He just needed to keep at it.

"You can also look at it this way. After I eliminate the rest of his men, Mallette's gonna be there in prison with nobody left to give orders to."

"And you think that would free me? All that means is that I'd be tasked with finding more recruits."

"But you don't have to. At that point you can just walk away."

"Walk away? And here I thought you knew Mallette better. Walking away is something someone doesn't do to him. You should know that. He'd have me killed out of spite or he'd turn evidence over to have me in prison next to him."

"So, you're just gonna accept things as they are?" Jacobs asked. "Let him drag you down into the gutter next to him?"

"I don't know if I've made this clear yet, but I don't have options."

"What if I told you I would protect you?"

"Very noble sentiment but one that I don't think is entirely practical," Wiggins said. "You see, while you're off playing superhero, little old me will at times be alone and vulnerable. You can't be in fifty places at once. But I appreciate the thought."

"Once he gets out of prison, he's as good as dead. You know that, right? Are you seriously gonna take a bullet alongside of him?"

Wiggins put his head in his hands, not knowing what to do. He really wanted to take Jacobs up on his offer but he was still deathly afraid of what Mallette would do to him if he found out. After some soul searching, he picked his head back up and stared at Jacobs for a moment. He almost didn't believe what was about to come out of his mouth.

"If...if I was to help you with this, how exactly am I going to prevent getting caught up in the crossfire of this little party you have planned?"

"Duck," Jacobs replied.

Wiggins laughed. "I must be out of my mind."

"I wouldn't doubt that."

Wiggins let out a deep breath, giving himself one last chance to back out of it before he did the unthinkable. He decided to go ahead with it. "Fine. I'll help you get these kids. And after that, I would hope that takes me off your radar for good."

"It will. Unless you take some other kids or try to kill me or something stupid like that."

"Not likely," Wiggins said. "To be honest, I'm getting kind of tired seeing your face."

Jacobs smiled. "That makes two of us."

"Oh, and there's one more thing. If after I do this for you, assuming you're still alive, if you ever hear of anything about Mallette finding out and coming after me, I'd appreciate it if you could stick your nose into it for me."

"You got my word on that," Jacobs said, extending his hand as the two men shook on the deal.

Wiggins then called his secretary and had her cancel any other appointments he had for the day as he and Jacobs spent the next twenty minutes or so going over the situation. After hearing the setup, Wiggins gave his input on what he thought would be best.

"I can call them and tell them Mallette has other business for them, effectively cut their numbers in half."

"That might make them think something's going on though," Jacobs said. "I don't wanna take chances of getting there and finding out the ones who left took the kids with them."

"I could instruct them to leave the kids there."

"Maybe. You don't think they might think something's up considering you already said you didn't wanna be a part of it?"

"Well, that was me. If I tell them Mallette's got something..."

"But will they know you haven't met with him again since he ordered this?"

"Hmm. That's a good point. They might question that."

"I say we just go in and deal with everything once we get there," Jacobs said.

"I'm still gonna have to call Wickers and have him tell me where we're going."

"Why?"

"Because I'm not supposed to know where he's at. If I just show up there unannounced he's going to know something's wrong for sure. Then I'll be dead before you even get in."

"Make it convincing."

Before calling, Wiggins quickly crafted a story to feed to Wickers, hoping that he'd buy it. Now that they agreed to call Wickers, they just had to hope that he'd pick up since he'd largely gone phone silent in the last few days. Their hope was that he'd pick up seeing that it was Wiggins, just in case he was delivering a message from Mallette. They were happily surprised to see that it worked as Wickers picked up on the second ring.

"Hey, what's up?" Wickers said.

"I was just calling to see how that little arrangement was going."

"I thought you didn't want to be involved in all that."

"I don't," Wiggins said. "But the boss does. He somehow pulled some strings to get an emergency meeting with me early this morning. Made it seem like we were discussing legal options on his case. Never mind that, though. He wants to know how it's going. And since I haven't seen or heard Jacobs' name on any obituary notices, I had no choice but to tell him it was going slowly. I don't have to tell you how well that went over. He was not very happy."

"I know, I know. We're working on it."

"That is not what he wants to hear," Wiggins replied, conveying an angry tone. "He wants to know specifics. He wants to know where you are, when this thing's going down, oh, and let's not forget, he wants to know why three more of his men were found dead in that office building last night."

Wickers sighed loudly into the phone, knowing he was in deep trouble. "It was just something we tried, hoping we could get the jump on Jacobs. It obviously didn't work."

"Obviously. Now do you have those kids or don't you?"

"We do."

"Fine. Where are you right now?"

"Antique shop."

"OK. So, what exactly is your plan for Jacobs?" Wiggins asked.

"We're gonna contact him tonight to have him come here. Then when he does, we take him out."

"Why later?"

"We'll contact him about thirty minutes before the meeting that way we know he doesn't have enough time to set up a trap of his own."

"Excellent. What about the kids? Are they alive?"

"For now."

Wiggins looked at Jacobs and nodded, giving him a thumbs up. "Fine. Keep them that way."

"Why? What difference does it make?"

"Because if you kill those kids and he somehow finds out about it, he's certainly not going to agree to come to your meeting, now is he?"

"How's he gonna find out?" Wickers asked.

"How does he do a lot of things? He's got inside sources, connections. I suspect he's doing a lot of things illegally... wiretapping, hacking, that sort of thing. You just keep playing things straight for now."

"OK."

"You guys just stay put for now. I'm on my way there. Text me the address once we're done."

"What? Why?"

"Because unfortunately for you, Mr. Mallette is not as confident about this situation as you seem to be. He's already hired outside help."

"Outside help? What?"

"Another contract with our friends from New York," Wiggins said.

"We don't need them."

"Regardless of what your opinion is, or mine for that matter, Mr. Mallette feels differently. He's not as sure as you are that you can adequately handle the situation. He feels you've already bungled things with your stunt last night."

"Hey, I got twelve guys here. We can handle it."

"It doesn't matter what you or I think. This other man has already been hired and is currently en route to my office. Mallette wants me to drive over to you personally and meet this man so he can be there when everything goes down. I'm gonna have to call him and tell him to change his itinerary and meet me where you're at."

"That's not necessary," Wickers repeated, feeling like his professional capabilities were being insulted.

"As I said, it's out of my hands as well as yours. This is coming from the top. You don't have to like it. You just have to do it. Understand?"

Wickers let out another loud sigh. "Yeah, yeah. OK."

"I will be there in one hour. Text me the address."

"Yeah, yeah, I'll text you the address."

Wiggins hung up and immediately looked to Jacobs. "Went as well as can be expected. He's not happy, but I think he bought it."

"You sure?"

"About as sure as anyone can be in this situation. He's as much afraid of disappointing or angering Mallette as anyone. He'll do whatever the boss wants."

Jacobs nodded, believing they just might be able to pull this off. "That's good. Maybe we'll live through this after all."

"That would be encouraging."

## 11

J acobs and Wiggins stayed in the office a few more minutes, trying to go over and perfect their plans more. As they were doing so, Wickers sent Wiggins a text with the address. He showed it to Jacobs, who nodded. It was the same address as the antique shop. It was only about a thirty-minute drive from the office to the store so they still had a little time before they had to go. As they were leaving, Jacobs called Franks to let him know the deal.

"All right, we just got confirmation from Wickers," Jacobs said. "They're at the antique shop with the kids."

"Confirmation from Wickers? How'd you manage that?"

"I told you. Wiggins is getting me in."

"Brett, you sure you can trust him?" Franks asked, still worried about him being double crossed.

"We've already been over that. It is what it is at this point. We just gotta roll with it."

"If you say so. So, what's the plan?"

"Wiggins told them he's bringing them a hired gun at Mallette's orders. That should be able to get me in."

"And then?"

"According to Wickers they got twelve guns in there," Jacobs said.

"Oh, nothing to it then."

"Stop being an old fusspot. I need you to close shop and start heading over there so you can be ready like we planned."

"And if you don't make it out?"

"Then I guess you don't have to wait."

Though still not happy about the plan, and not convinced that it would work, Franks did as was requested and closed the store down. Luckily, he didn't have any customers, not that it would have mattered, as he would have shooed them out quickly anyway. He was closer to the antique shop than Jacobs was and wound up getting there a few minutes earlier. Jacobs and Wiggins drove down together in the lawyer's car, continuing to shape their plan, which seemed to be in constant flux, as they kept changing things. When they were only a few minutes away, they finally finalized their plan. Wiggins stopped the car only a block away and let Jacobs out, who was going to approach the building from the back. Once Wiggins was inside, he'd make his way to the back and let him in. As Jacobs got out, he reached into his bag and pulled out his base-ball hat and pulled it down to try and conceal his face. It'd be pivotal if he hoped to get inside the building unscathed.

By the time Wiggins pulled in front of the former antique business, it was exactly one hour from his conversation with Wickers. He got out and took a quick look around to see if anything looked strange, but everything seemed as normal as it could be under the circumstances. He started walking to the door and noticed a few faces looking out of it, though he couldn't quite make out who it was. All he could tell was that it appeared to be two or three people. As he got closer to it, the door opened slightly, not opening fully until Wiggins was almost on top of it. As the men made themselves visible, Wiggins instantly recognized all of them. Wickers wasn't among them.

As Wiggins walked inside, one of the men stepped out and looked up and down the street to make sure they had no unwelcome visitors. Once he saw they were clear, he stepped back inside, closing and locking the door behind him. Wiggins walked to the middle of the room, then stopped, looking the place over. He noticed stairs along the far wall that led up to the second floor, complete with a railing that went along the edge of it and overlooked the first floor. As Wiggins looked around, he observed four men on the first floor including those who greeted him at the door. As he looked above him, he saw four more men with their arms on the railing looking down at him. But there was something missing.

"I don't see Wickers," Wiggins said. "Where is he?"

"Oh, he left a few minutes ago."

"Left? Why? What for? I told him I was coming. I expect him to be here."

The man shrugged. "I dunno. He didn't say. He just took four of the boys, along with the kids, and said maybe he'd be back later."

"He took the kids?"

"Yeah."

"And he didn't say why or where he was going?"

"He didn't. Just grabbed them and left."

"Was he talking to someone after me?" Wiggins asked. "Get a phone call or anything?"

"No, not that I saw."

"The boss isn't gonna be happy that he's not here."

"I told him to stick around, but he just ignored me and left. Said he'd be back."

"He say what time?"

"Nope."

"All right, well, we can't waste anymore time waiting for him," Wiggins said, knowing he soon had to let Jacobs in.

They gave themselves no more than five minutes after Wiggins arrived for him to let Jacobs in. If Jacobs wasn't let in within five minutes then he was to assume that the plan failed and that Wiggins was in some sort of trouble. If that was the case, then Jacobs would have to move around to the front and come in guns blazing.

"Thought you were supposed to be bringing somebody," the man said. "Wickers mentioned something about another guy from New York."

"Yes, he should be here momentarily. He told me he'd just meet me here."

"Another hotshot who can't do the job any better than we can?"

"Yeah, well, we'll see," Wiggins said. "I better see if he's here. Said he'd come through the back. Didn't want to take the chance of being spotted by anybody walking along out front."

"Makes sense, I guess."

Wiggins then went to the back door. He looked over his shoulder to see if any of the others were following him. Much to his delight, they were not. At least part of their plan was working. With the kids, along with Wickers and the others no longer there, it wouldn't be a total victory no matter what Jacobs did. But from Wiggins' point of view, not encountering any problems was a big accomplishment, especially for his personal safety. He took one more look behind him before opening the door. The others were just standing around talking to each other. It didn't look like they would be a problem.

Wiggins opened the door and looked for Jacobs, quickly seeing the top of his head, only his face visible as he squatted between two parked cars. He then motioned for him to come over. A fleeting thought came over Jacobs as he approached the building, wondering about being set-up and whether there would be ten guns staring at him once he got to the door. He shrugged it off, though, having faith that Wiggins was as interested in breaking free of Mallette's clutches as Jacobs thought he was. Once he got to the door, Wiggins stepped out a little further so he wasn't in plain view of the men inside in case they were watching.

"There's only eight men here," Wiggins said. "Wickers and some others left with the kids about ten or twenty minutes ago. No idea why."

A dejected look overcame Jacobs' face. "Figures."

"Still wanna do this?"

"Already here. Might as well."

"Then you should know there's four on the first floor, middle of the room. The other four are on the second floor. Stairs are off to the side of the room. There's a balcony overlooking the bottom level and I noticed a couple of the guys were up against the railing so watch out for that."

"Thanks for the info."

Even though the kids weren't there, going back didn't even enter Jacobs' mind. He came there to not only get the kids, but also to take out more of Mallette's men. That part of the equation wasn't going to change regardless of who wasn't there. It was an opportunity to shrink Mallette's Maulers even more, and he was going to seize that opportunity.

"You need me for anything else?" Wiggins asked.

"No, get out of here."

Wiggins wasted no time in running around the building to get back to his car. Jacobs walked inside and let the door close behind him. He kept his hat pulled down tight to his eyes to try and prevent being recognized, wanting to get closer to his targets before the chaos began. The four men on the first level stopped talking as the man came closer.

"You the new guy?"

"Sure am," Jacobs said, getting as close as he needed to.

Jacobs then reached inside his coat with both hands and removed his guns. With the amount of men he was facing, he figured it was best to start firing with two guns at once. He immediately pointed his weapons at the two men on the outside of the group, shooting them point blank in the chest. As they hit the ground, Jacobs re-aimed toward the two inside men, also hitting them before they had a chance to remove their own guns.

Remembering what Wiggins told him about the balcony, Jacobs quickly spun around and looked up at the railing, seeing one man with a gun in his hand. The man fired at Jacobs, though the bullet missed its target. Jacobs returned fire, hitting the man several times. The man lunged forward, flipping over the top of the railing, making a thunderous bang on the floor as his body came to a rest.

Jacobs looked back at the second floor, though he didn't see anyone. He figured they must have retreated to another spot up there. He took another look at the five bodies lying around him and noticed three of them were still moving. He couldn't leave them alive and risk them coming up behind him if he was on the second floor or had his back turned to them. He had to eliminate them. He fired two more shots into each of their bodies, ending their lives instantly.

Jacobs stepped over a couple of the bodies and rushed over to the bottom of the stairs. He stood there for a minute, hoping one of the remaining men would show their face at the top of it so he could shoot it off. He had no such luck. He imagined they were doing the same thing, waiting for him to show his face at the top so they could shoot him when he showed his face. He figured he had two choices at that point. Either continue with the task at hand and risk getting shot or just pack up and leave, content that he at least knocked off five more of Mallette's men. If it weren't for the kids' lives being at stake, there was a good chance Jacobs would have just left, content with his work, ready to save the battle for another day. But as it were, he couldn't chance it now. The thought occurred to him that maybe the kids really were there. Maybe they were just telling Wiggins they weren't to see his reaction in case they didn't fully trust him. Jacobs realized that it was probably a long shot, and the kids really weren't there, but he still had to make sure. He had to check.

With three men on the second floor, Jacobs knew they could have been anywhere, and they might have spread themselves out, hoping to ambush him somewhere. What made it even tougher was that Jacobs didn't know what the layout of the floor was. There were no pictures of the top floor from what Hack discovered. So, he was going in blind. Jacobs quietly crawled up the steps, being careful to not make any noises, though they were old steps and did creak a little. He wasn't getting up there by complete surprise. If the men were carefully listening, they would definitely hear the creaking of the stairs. But Jacobs didn't have any other choices. He couldn't engage in a stand-off, waiting there for hours to see who could hold out longer. He just didn't have that kind of time.

Jacobs continued his slow climb up the stairs in what seemed to take forever. Part of him hoped that the other three would get impatient and show themselves before he got there. That didn't happen, though. Once he finally reached near the top, he stopped a couple of steps below it, just to take a few extra seconds to collect his thoughts and not rush into anything. He climbed the remaining steps and raised his head just enough for his eyes to see. As soon as he did, though, a shot rang out. The bullet hit the floor right in front of Jacobs' face, missing him by only centimeters. Pieces of the wood flew up into his face, dust getting into his eyes. He slid back down a step as he wiped the debris out of his eyes, still trying to stay alert in case they came closer to try and take advantage of him.

Now he knew that they were up there waiting for him to show himself. But he didn't know if all three were or just one. He supposed it didn't really matter since they all had to be dealt with, though it would have been nice if he knew what direction they were all in. Jacobs took a few deep breaths, then jumped up from his position, hoping to catch them by surprise. He immediately noticed the one man in the corner and fired several rounds that hit the man, all before the man could return fire. He was not as lucky, however, with the other two men. While he was involved with the first man, the other two opened fire, both successfully hitting him.

The force of the blows knocked Jacobs backwards. He lost his balance and stumbled down the steps, violently rolling down until he stopped at the bottom of them, resting on the floor. He was lying on his side with his eyes closed. The two men looked down at him from above, one from the railing, the other at the top of the steps. They didn't observe Jacobs moving at all and they couldn't tell if he was still breathing.

"I think we got him," one said excitedly.

The other man didn't reply at first, trying to catch

his breath while not taking his eyes off the dangerous man. "We'll go down and take a look."

The two men started descending the stairs, walking slowly in case Jacobs was playing possum. They still had their guns firmly entrenched in their hands, arms pointing out, ready to fire again in quick fashion should the need arise. Once they got near the bottom, the one man motioned to the other to check on Jacobs' condition.

"Make sure he's dead. I'll cover you."

The man who was going to check on him licked his lips, then wiped his mouth, a little nervous about moving closer to the infamous man. Though Jacobs appeared to be dead, it was still a nerve-wracking experience being so close to him. Jacobs had his right arm tucked underneath his body, so neither of Mallette's men could see that he still had a gun glued to the fingers of his hand. As the man reached down to check on him, Jacobs opened his eyes wide. Seeing that he was still alive, the man let out a scream and jumped back. But as he was moving back, Jacobs spun his body around onto his back and blew a hole through the man's chest. Immediately after firing, Jacobs quickly turned his gun towards the other man and also put a bullet through him before he was able to get a shot off.

Jacobs kept his gun pointed at them for a few more seconds before realizing they were both dead. Knowing there was nobody else left for him to fight, he let out a deep sigh, then slumped his shoulders as he lay flat on his back, his head thumping on the hard-wood floor. A small sense of relief passed through him, satisfied at how things went, though he only allowed himself to feel happy for a brief few seconds before turning his thoughts back to the kids. As he lay there, Jacobs put his hands on his chest, feeling his bullet-proof vest where the bullets struck him at the top of the stairs.

"Guess this thing paid off," he whispered.

Though his body would have liked him to remain there for a while longer, he knew he had to go. There was no telling if police were on their way or not and Jacobs didn't want to be there when they arrived. He stood up, slightly wobbling and off balance, though he still started walking toward the back door, shrugging off that his legs felt like Jell-O and his chest felt like an elephant was standing on it. He called Franks just before he got there.

"Eddie, where you at?"

"Ready to go?" Franks asked.

"By the time you get here, you'll be late."

"On my way."

Franks peeled out of his spot and raced toward the building. In their plans, Jacobs was supposed to be out front, clinging to the side of the building as Franks got there. But due to all the chaos, and possibly from being shot and having his head bounced around as he fell down the stairs, Jacobs must have gotten confused and went out the back. He stood outside in plain view, in the middle of the lot, waiting for his friend to pick him up. Luckily, Franks came zooming in only a few seconds later. After not seeing Jacobs in front, Franks assumed that going out the front wasn't possible and figured that he was waiting in the back. As Franks stopped the car, the door swung open, Jacobs quickly getting in. As they drove away, Franks looked over and noticed that Jacobs was holding the back of his head.

"You all right?"

"Yeah. Nothing a bottle of aspirin won't cure," Jacobs replied.

"I see you got no cargo. What happened?"

"Kids aren't there. Neither was Wickers. Wiggins said they must've left about ten or twenty minutes before we got there."

"Think they got spooked?"

"Maybe. Not enough for all of them to go through so I'm not sure."

"Any ideas?" Franks asked.

Jacobs' hand switched from the back of his head to his forehead, rubbing it. "I don't know."

"Guess I was wrong about Wiggins."

"He came through like he said he would."

"So, what now?"

"I dunno. We're gonna have to go back and regroup. We're gonna have to find another way."

"After Wickers hears about what happened, he ain't gonna be easy to find," Franks said. "He's gonna dig a hole real deep."

"I know. We're just gonna have to find a way."

"I know you don't wanna hear this, but it's also possible he gets scared off and just cuts bait."

"Meaning he kills the kids?" Jacobs asked.

"I'm just saying."

"And I'm just saying...we can't let that happen. We gotta find them.

## 12

After a brief stop at Jacobs' house for him to clean up, and get Gunner, they went back to the pawn shop to go over their next course of action. Hack was still there banging away on the keyboard, much to the surprise of both Jacobs and Franks, who both thought he'd be gone by now.

"What are you still doing here?" Franks asked. "Thought you had to be somewhere?"

"Well, yeah, I did, but I canceled," Hack replied. "It wasn't anything important anyway. This is where I need to be right now."

Jacobs put his hand on Hack's shoulder. "Appreciate that, bud."

"Hey, whatever I can do to help."

"Get any hits on Wickers after he left the antique shop?"

"No, not so far. I've tried to trace his phone after the

phone call from Wiggins, but I lost it. The signal's not active anymore so he either turned it off, or threw it away, or broke it...something along those lines."

"Any known hangouts?"

"I mean, nothing that we haven't checked into before when we first started looking for him," Hack said.

"We need to do something different."

"Thought that's what Wiggins was about," Franks said.

"It was."

"Well, that didn't work either."

"Worked fine," Jacobs said. "Took out eight of his guys. Just didn't find what we were hoping for."

The three men sat down and threw some ideas around before Jacobs thought of Wiggins again. Franks didn't like going to him again, figuring they were over-stepping their welcome.

"How many times you think you can go to the well?" Franks asked.

"Until it dries up," Jacobs answered.

"You really think there's anything else he can tell you?"

Jacobs shrugged. "Guess we'll find out."

Jacobs turned to Hack again to get Wiggins' phone number. He had written down his cell phone and business numbers before Jacobs' first visit to the lawyer. Hack found the paper and slid it over to him. Jacobs immediately dialed Wiggins' cell phone since he wasn't sure if he had gone back to the office.

"Lawrence Wiggins here."

"Hey, it's Jacobs."

"Oh no," Wiggins said, figuring the call could only be bad news. "Well., considering you're calling, I'm assuming you made it out of there alive."

"Good assumption."

"The rest of them dead?"

"Yep."

"Do you need me to jump out of a burning building next? Or how about a moving train? Parachute jumping without the parachute? Or maybe walk across a bed of nails? What other torture do you have in mind for me?"

Jacobs couldn't help but be amused. "That's actually kind of funny."

"For you maybe."

"I actually don't need you for any of that. Just wanted to say thanks for what you did earlier. Even though it didn't go quite as I planned or hoped, still wasn't a total loss."

"For you maybe."

"What do you mean?" Jacobs asked.

"Well, it's an absolute disaster for me."

"How so?"

"Seems as though I'm in pretty deep now. You didn't get what you wanted, Wickers escaped with the children, and he's probably thinking that I double-crossed him. Which means Mallette will know it soon enough."

"Not if we get to Wickers first."

"The only reason he would have left was if he was having some doubts about me," Wiggins said. "Those doubts will only have intensified after hearing about what happened."

"Mallette only sees one visitor a week and that's you, right? How's he gonna hear about anything unless you're the one who tells him?"

"Please, we both know the prison system is corrupt and information can flow in and out of that place somewhat freely. If you honestly believe the only way Mallette gets information is from me, you're sadly mistaken. And someone dumber than I initially thought."

"Well, then help me get to him before he's able to get a message through," Jacobs said.

"Haven't we already been there, done that?"

"He couldn't have gone too far. If you can figure out any other places that he might have gone that'd be a big help."

"I'm not sure. He's never been a guy who I conversed with much outside of transferring informa- tion to and from Mallette."

Jacobs was silent for a few seconds as he thought of alternatives. Nothing was coming to him. He thought about having Wiggins contact Wickers again, but then remembered what Hack said about Wickers' phone being off the grid. Then he thought of a similar idea.

"There could be one other thing," Jacobs said.

Wiggins sighed, knowing he probably wouldn't like it as he only seemed to be getting himself in deeper the more he threw in with Jacobs. "What is it?"

"Contact Wickers again."

"Are you crazy? I wouldn't be surprised if he kills me the moment he sees me."

"Not if we turn the tables on him. Make him think what he thinks isn't what happened at all."

"I'm sure there's some sense in what you just said, but I'm failing to see it."

"From what I can gather, Wickers' phone is off," Jacobs said. "Do you know who else you could call to get in touch with him. Three others left with him from the antique shop."

"Well, there's one or two others he hangs out with more than others. I'm sure it wouldn't take long to figure out which one of those are with him."

"Then get in touch with him through them."

"And say what exactly?"

"Make it seem like you're shocked and stunned by what happened. Tell him you got there and found everyone dead."

"He'll never believe that," Wiggins said.

"Won't know unless you try."

"Listen, he won't go for it. And how do you know he wasn't watching the festivities from a nearby place?"

"I dunno. Just seems like that'd be a stupid thing to do. One little slip-up, one of the kids yells, something gives his location away, and I'm right in his face. No, I think as soon as he left, he probably got away as far as he could. At least until he figured out what was going on."

"Well, it's a cinch that he didn't go back to the antique shop again with the kids, but you can bet that he sent someone back there to check," Wiggins said.

"Why do you suppose he got jumpy and left?"

"Who knows? Could have been anything. Maybe he didn't believe the thing about bringing in a New York guy again."

"So, can you try and call him?" Jacobs asked.

"You're intent on getting me killed, aren't you?"

"I wouldn't be asking if there weren't kids involved."

"Yeah, I'll call, though I don't think it's going to do any good. He obviously doesn't trust me anymore."

"Make him doubt it. Make him think he's being paranoid. You're a lawyer, you can talk good and spin around the truth. You wouldn't be Mallette's lawyer if you couldn't."

"Is that a backhanded compliment?"

"I thought it was more the forehand, but you can take it however you like."

"Very funny."

"So, you'll do it?" Jacobs asked.

"Yes. Give me a number where I can reach you."

"How 'bout I just call you again in twenty minutes?"

"Afraid I'll turn the tables on you?"

"If there's one thing I've learned, it's that you can never be too trusting."

"Fair enough."

Once they hung up, Jacobs put his phone down and looked at the others, who were eagerly awaiting word on what was going on.

"So?" Franks asked. "What's happening?"

"Wiggins is gonna try and get in touch with Wickers again."

"I'm afraid that ship's sailed, my friend. No way he's gonna talk to Wiggins again. If he does, there's no way he'll give him any factual information. Probably tell him he's clear on the other side of town."

"Even if he does, maybe there'll be something we can use. It's worth a shot."

Franks agreed that there was probably no harm in trying, though he was skeptical they'd get anything useful out of it. Wiggins had just gotten back to his house a few minutes before Jacobs had called. He was sitting at his kitchen table as he started placing calls to friends of Wickers. It was a small list at this point as Jacobs had taken out most of Mallette's Maulers. In fact, there were only about twelve members left, including the four that now had his brother's kids.

One by one, they all told Wiggins that they hadn't heard of Wickers' whereabouts lately. And none admitted to talking to him recently. Wiggins knew that a few of them were probably lying, and at least one of them was probably standing next to Wickers as they were talking, but had to play the game their way. He knew his reputation was in serious peril with the remaining members of the group after the antique shop. Especially after Wiggins' phone was spoofed, directing people to the Mallette warehouse, where Jacobs gunned down a bunch of them before. That was when the doubts started creeping in about Wiggins amongst the group members. And though most accepted the story that Jacobs had rigged his phone, there were still a few who never fully accepted the story and wondered about Wiggins' loyalty. This latest incident would be the last straw for them. Even if he was innocent, the rest of the Maulers would never fully trust him again.

After he finished calling the rest of the group, Wiggins poured himself a good stiff drink. Regardless of Jacobs' assurances, he knew word would probably get to Mallette within a couple of days at the latest. And if Mallette agreed with them that Wiggins was the weak link and helping Jacobs, the order would go out to have him terminated. He started thinking about running, wondering if he could pull it off. He had a good amount of money saved up. Maybe he could go to some foreign country or maybe some island some-where and try to live the rest of his life in obscurity. Even if Mallette sent someone looking for him, he'd probably have at least a week or two head start. He thought he just might be able to pull it off.

Wiggins poured himself a couple more drinks before he finally was able to convince himself that he could actually slip away from everybody. He got out his laptop and started looking up destinations where he thought he could hide. Somewhere outside of the United States. After about twenty minutes of searching, and with his mind almost completely made up, his phone started ringing. It was one of the men he'd just called. One of Wickers' friends. Now that he'd decided to blow the area, the thought occurred to Wiggins to just ignore it. Nothing that was said now would matter or make any kind of difference to him. Then he thought of the kids of Jacobs' brother. He closed his eyes and mumbled under his breath for caring at all about them. He thought of his own kids. Even though he was divorced and didn't see them often, he still had a soft spot for them. Even kids who weren't his own. He wanted to kick himself for what he was about to do. He quickly reached down and picked up the phone before it stopped ringing.

"Yes?" Wiggins said.

"Hey, you still wanna talk to Wickers?"

"Yes, I do."

"He's right here, hold on."

The phone then passed to Wickers, who got on, a little hot under the collar. "You got a lot of explaining to do, hotshot."

"Me?" Wiggins asked. "Perhaps you'd like to explain how Jacobs found out where you were?"

"I need to explain?"

"Yes, you need to explain. I showed up at the antique store with our friend from New York and when I looked inside all I saw were dead bodies. What exactly happened out there?"

"You tell me."

"Like I said, I arrived there with our friend from New York, just like we agreed. When I stepped inside, I saw a lot of bodies lying on the floor. I noticed you were not among them, the kids weren't there, that's when I started calling around. How did you get out?"

Though Wickers was initially peeved, he was starting to calm down. There was no doubt in his mind at first that Wiggins was playing both sides of the fence. But now he wasn't so sure. He didn't factor in this phone call and Wiggins acting like he knew nothing of what happened. The thought occurred to Wickers that maybe the lawyer was being played again, just like what happened at the warehouse when Steckenridge bought it. Maybe he really didn't have a hand in it. Sensing Wickers' hesitation, Wiggins tried to keep up the snow job to really sell it.

"I didn't see Jacobs' body there, what happened to him? Did he escape, did you hit him, what?" Wiggins asked.

"Uh, I don't know. We cut out early."

"You did what? You had Jacobs in your grasps, just

as the plan called for, and you left early? How do you expect me to sell that to Mallette?"

"I had a bad feeling about things after you called," Wickers said. "I thought it best not to be there."

"You would have had him outnumbered twelve to one. How could you do that?"

Wickers started questioning himself, wondering if he had done the wrong thing. "I just thought..."

"You're not paid to think. You're paid to follow orders and then execute them. Not go off half-baked with your own stupid ideas. Now we have eight more men dead. We don't have an endless supply, you know. If you would have just stayed put we could have put an end to this situation. Now we got to figure out a new plan."

"We still have the kids and we still have him outnumbered."

"We couldn't take him out with eight men, you really expect you four idiots will be able to?" Wiggins asked, laying it on thick. "We don't even have the kids to use as leverage anymore."

"What do you mean? They're still alive. I haven't done anything to them yet."

"That's not the point. The point of this whole exercise was to give Jacobs overwhelming odds and present him with a situation where he had to give up and surrender to us. Make him lose his will to fight. That obviously has not happened and won't. Against twelve men, he was supposed to feel like he couldn't win and to trade his life for those kids. Now, he knows he's going against significantly less odds and doesn't have to do that. He knows he can fight and scheme and plan against us. You've really bungled this."

"Hey, you're the one who said you didn't wanna be a part of this," Wickers replied angrily. "You're the one who left it on me to figure out what to do. So, don't hang this on me. Maybe Mr. Mallette won't like it so much that you bailed out on this."

"Sitting here and arguing with each other and playing the blame game isn't going to change the situation at this point. Let's calm down and figure out what to do from here. Where are you right now? Maybe I can come down and we'll put our heads together."

"No offense, counselor, but you're not exactly at the top of my trusted friends. Even if I believe you, how do I know he didn't follow you or have you tailed? Or maybe he's got your phone bugged or something?"

Wiggins knew he couldn't push too hard or he'd risk coming off like he really was in Jacobs' pocket. "Hmm, you may have a point there. I can't say for certain that he doesn't have me bugged or tailed or something. Sounds like something he's capable of."

"I'll figure something out on my own," Wickers said. "Tell Mr. Mallette I've got it handled."

"At least tell me you're not somewhere that Jacobs can find you again. Not at one of our known hangouts."

"Don't worry. I made arrangements before this to

get another place in case the antique store didn't work out."

"Fine. What's your plan to lure Jacobs there?"

"Same as before. We'll contact him later and tell him where to come."

"Oh, that sounds perfect," Wiggins sarcastically said. "Can't see anything going wrong there. Honestly, you might as well let the kids go at this point. There's no need to hold them any longer."

"They're our insurance."

"Really? Can you be any more stupid? Listen, Jacobs is coming for you now whether you have the kids or not. It might be more beneficial for you to cut them loose so you can focus on Jacobs. He is your main focus. Those kids mean nothing. He was just a way to draw him in. Now that this whole thing's been bungled, he's coming regardless."

Wickers thought about it, but still felt they were better off holding the kids. "Uh, I think we'll keep them anyway. Just in case."

"Well, suit yourself. I'll leave that to you. I'll expect you to call me tomorrow with news that Jacobs is dead."

"That will be a call I'll have no problem making," Wickers said.

"Well, we will see about that. Oh, and one more thing."

"Yeah?"

"Make sure those kids live through this."

"Why? What's it matter?"

"Mr. Mallette only wanted them harmed if it would somehow hurt Jacobs," Wiggins said. "If Jacobs is dead, then that is obviously no longer a concern. He's not out to hurt children on a whim."

"Well, we'll just see how the night goes."

They then hung up, Wiggins confident in how he handled the situation, feeling like he was now in control again. He had a firm grip on things. He thought that he adequately convinced Wickers that he wasn't involved in the antique shop incident. There was nothing else he could do for Jacobs to help get the kids, but for his own selfish point of view, he felt he didn't need to run now. Since he wasn't trying to make getaway plans anymore, he turned his computer off and went over to his couch to put his feet up and relax. He was now starting to feel pretty good about his situation. He had Wickers in check; he didn't feel threatened by Mallette knowing anything, and he had Jacobs' word that he wouldn't be touched again. He didn't feel it could have worked out any better. Wiggins started to doze off on the couch but was woken up by the phone ringing again.

"Just checking in," Jacobs said. "Anybody get back to you yet?"

"Actually, yes. I just had a conversation with Wickers."

"How'd it go?"

"Well, good and bad, depending on one's point of view."

"How about my point of view?"

"I'd say you'll probably view it as one of those glass half full or empty type of deals," Wiggins said.

"I never like those."

"Well, the good news is the kids are still alive."

"And the bad news?" Jacobs asked.

"I still don't know where he is."

"What else did he say?"

"Well, he'll be contacting you later to set up a new meet," Wiggins said. "He also mentioned that he's not in a place that's familiar to Mallette's businesses."

"You sure he was being honest in everything he told you?"

"Yes, I believe so. I believe I successfully convinced him that I didn't know what happened at the antique store. I showed up and everyone was dead. But, that leads him to believe that I might be followed or tailed, or have a phone bugged or something, so that's about all the help I can be to you anymore. Even if he doesn't believe I was directly involved, he doesn't trust me now if he believes you're on my tail."

"That means he didn't stick around after leaving."

"No, but he knew what happened, which leads me to believe he sent someone back."

"I kind of figured that."

"I did what I could for you," Wiggins said. "I tried to get him to release the kids, saying they'd be a detriment to them when they needed to focus on you, but it didn't work. He's going to keep them anyway."

"Well, you tried. That's about all I could ask. I thank you for that."

"I guess that will conclude our business? Unless you still need me to jump out of that plane or something?"

"No, I think we're good."

"In saying that, I wish you luck, and hopefully we'll never see or talk to each other again."

"Oh, you don't wanna hang out anymore?" Jacobs sarcastically asked. "That hurts my feelings."

"I bet. Good luck."

Jacobs at least found some solace in knowing that the kids were still alive, which was always his greatest concern. Now he just had to find them again. Although he knew it was possible to do that, he had a feeling it wouldn't be as easy this time around. Nevertheless, they had to try. After putting his phone down, he turned to the others and told them the information he got from Wiggins.

"What do you think?" Jacobs asked.

"We can do it," Hack replied. "I'll find him again."

"Maybe focus on the brother again," Franks said. "If he got him one place, he might have gotten him another."

Jacobs turned his head away in thought. Franks could tell something was going through his mind.

"What are you thinking?" Franks asked.

"Maybe we can do two things at once."

"Meaning?"

"Meaning that while you guys run things down on your end, I'll take a different approach."

"Again, meaning?"

"Meaning that maybe I'll have a little chat with Addison Wickerson," Jacobs said. "Maybe there's more that he could tell us."

"A little chat, huh?"

Jacobs smiled. "Something to that effect."

## 13

While Hack tried to run down other leads, hoping to find another instance of Wickerson renting out a building for his brother, Jacobs went to pay the man a visit. Once he got to Wickerson's house, there were no cars parked and no lights on. Nothing that would indicate anyone was there. It looked like Jacobs would have to wait a little while. In normal circumstances, he wouldn't have minded the wait so much, but these weren't normal circumstances. And he really didn't have time to wait. Then he got an idea on how to get Wickers back to the house quickly. He called Franks to have him enact his part of it.

"What's the word?" Franks asked.

"Looks like Wickerson's not here."

"What are you gonna do? Wait?"

"Not exactly what I had in mind. I was hoping

Hack could get his number, then you call him and get him to come back to the house."

"How do you expect me to do that?"

"I dunno. Tell him you're a cop or something and that his house was burglarized and that you need him to come down now."

"And you think that'll work?"

"You can be convincing," Jacobs said. "Make it work."

"The things I do for you. All right, I'll give it a go."

"I'll eagerly await your call."

"Smartass."

Once Franks hung up, he got Wickerson's cell phone number from Hack and immediately started dialing. He didn't want to take too long to place the call or think about it too much. He thought he often did some of his best work on the fly when he didn't have much time to prepare. Luckily, Wickerson picked up after only a couple of rings.

"Hello?"

"Yeah, is this Addison Wickerson?" Franks asked.

"Yes, it is, who's this?"

"This is Detective Frankson of the Chicago Police Department."

"OK? What can I do for you?"

"Well, I'm calling to let you know there's been a robbery at your home a little while ago," Franks said. "We're at the scene now and need you to come down to identify what's missing so we can get it in our report."

"Uh, yeah, yeah, I'll be right there. Probably take me about fifteen, twenty minutes."

"We'll be here." After Franks put the phone down, he turned to Hack. "That went a lot easier than I thought it would."

Hack smiled. "Maybe you missed your calling. Maybe you should've gone to the police academy."

"Are you kidding? Way too much work for that. Plus, I hear the pay's not so great."

Franks then called Jacobs to let him know the target was on his way. When the phone rang, Jacobs was a little surprised that it was so soon.

"I wasn't expecting you to call back already," Jacobs said.

"What do you expect from the ol' master?"

"You get him?"

"Pfft, please. As if you have to question."

"So, what's the deal?"

"Wickerson should be there in about fifteen minutes so be ready," Franks said.

"I'll be ready."

"Hey, you know, this whole cop thing was actually kind of cool. Made me feel important."

"I bet. Just don't get too used to it," Jacobs said.

"Well, at least now we know I can pull it off if I ever have to do it again."

"I'll keep it in mind."

Having more time to wait, Jacobs continued sitting in his car for another ten minutes. As the fifteen-minute mark approached, Jacobs got out of the car and walked to the front door of Wickerson's house. He looked at it for a second and thought he'd give the appearance a little more realism. He wanted to make sure that Wickerson wouldn't have any apprehensions as he came to the house. If he saw that his house had no signs of burglary, with only one man standing there and no police cars in the area, Jacobs thought that might make him panic, or at least make the situation more difficult.

Jacobs thought about trying to kick the door in, but it looked like a heavy-duty door, and he didn't want to stand there forever trying to kick it open. He didn't want it to look suspicious to any nosy neighbors. With that in mind, he went to the nearest window and took a quick look around to make sure nobody was watching. He took out his gun and smashed the window with it. Only a few minutes later, another car rolled up. A middle-aged man got out, Jacobs recognizing Wickerson from his picture.

"I expected there to be a lot more of you here under the circumstances," Wickerson said.

"Well, we're not exactly sure there's a problem."

"Oh? You Frankson?"

"Who?" Jacobs asked.

"Frankson. The guy who called me on the phone. He said there was a robbery. You him?"

"Oh, yeah. No, that's not me."

"Then what's this about?"

Jacobs then pointed to the smashed window, with the pieces of glass on the ground. "Well, we don't know for sure there was a robbery. One of your neighbors reported seeing someone here, so we responded and found this. As you can see, it certainly looks like someone broke in. That's why we needed you to come down and confirm whether anything's missing or not. If there is, we can get started working on it. If not, then we'll just chalk it up to some mischief."

"Oh, OK," Wickerson said, walking to the door and putting his key in the lock.

Immediately after opening the door, Wickerson put his hand on the wall to feel for the light switch. Not seconds after flicking the lights on, Jacobs walloped Wickerson in the back of the head with his gun, sending the man flailing to the ground. Jacobs closed the door to make sure nothing could be heard, though he didn't account for the open window that he just created. Wickerson grabbed the back of his head and rolled around for a bit before turning over onto his back as he looked up at his attacker.

"What the hell, man?"

"Sorry," Jacobs said, though not the least bit apologetic.

"You're not a cop. What's this all about?"

Jacobs didn't answer at first and walked around his body, locating a small chair by the kitchen table. He dragged it over to the middle of the room.

"Sit."

"I think you gave me a concussion or something," Wickerson said, still holding his head, taking his time in complying with the directive.

"Sit," Jacobs replied, more forcefully.

Wickerson thought maybe he was lucky that he just had a nasty bump on his head at that point and figured he should do what was asked of him before something worse happened. Jacobs slowly walked around him as Wickerson pulled himself onto the chair.

"What do you want with me?" Wickerson asked. "I don't have drugs or money if that's what you're after."

"It's not what I'm after."

"Then what do you want?"

"I'm after some specific information that I think you can provide."

"Like what?"

"I'll get to it. First, I wanna lay down some ground rules here," Jacobs said. "I'm gonna ask you some questions and you're gonna tell me the answers. I want the truth and I better get it. If I do get it, you might just walk out of here alive. If I don't, and you're snow-jobbing me, or I think you're lying to me, I'll kill you right here. You understand?"

Wickerson, looking nervous, wiped the sweat off his forehead with his hand. "Yes."

"You talk to your brother lately?"

"Johnny? Yeah. A few days ago."

"You two close?"

Wickerson shrugged. "Eh, not that much."

"Then why did you go out and rent a building for him?"

Wickerson looked stunned. "How'd you know that?"

"Doesn't matter. What does matter is whether you know what he's up to?"

Wickerson wasn't quite sure how to respond, not knowing what was being referred to since it sounded like a loaded question. "Uh, I'm not sure what you mean."

"Do you know what he wanted the building for?"

"Yeah, he wanted to try and start his own business."

Jacobs raised his eyebrows, knowing what a load of crap that was. Now he had to figure out whether Wickerson actually believed that or if he was trying to determine how gullible he was. "His own business, huh?"

"Yeah, that's what he said. Why?"

"You know he works for Mallette's Maulers?"

"I know he did for a while, but he told me he was done with that," Wickerson said. "Listen, I know my brother hasn't always been a great guy, he's had his share of trouble with the law, and believe me, we've also had our share of problems over the years, but he said he was trying to get away from all that."

"So, why'd you sign the lease?"

"He said he was having a hard time making a go of it with his record. Nobody wanted to give him a chance. So, he asked if I would be willing to put everything in my name for a few months to see if he could make a go of it."

"Just out of the goodness of your heart?"

"What do you want? He's my brother. He came to me for help and I helped him."

"Well, I don't know about all that, but I can tell you what he really wanted that building for, and it ain't to start his own business."

Wickerson stared at his attacker, bracing himself for something that he knew he probably wasn't prepared to hear. A lump went down his throat as he waited for a further explanation.

"Regardless of what your brother told you, he's still working for Rich Mallette." Wickerson closed his eyes and sighed, knowing his brother probably played him. "And that building you signed a lease for, right now has eight dead bodies in it."

Wickerson shook his head and his eyes got a little glossy as he thought about his brother's troubles. "I, uh, guess I should've known. I knew it sounded too good to be true. He never expressed much remorse before or sounded like he ever wanted anything to be different. Then when he called me and said he was ready to start something different, make something better of his life, I just jumped at the chance. I probably would've believed anything he told me."

Jacobs nodded, getting the feeling that Wickerson was being genuine. "There's more to it than just that."

"Of course there is," Wickerson said dejectedly.

"Your brother's holding three kids hostage on Rich Mallette's orders and is planning on killing them if certain conditions aren't met."

Wickerson looked horrified. "No, my brother wouldn't do that."

"He would and he did. Three kids. Two boys and a girl. He's already admitted it. He was using that building you signed for as a meeting place for an exchange. I went there to get those kids. They were already gone, split just a few minutes before I got there along with your brother and three other men."

Wickerson leaned forward in his chair and put his elbows on his knees and hung his head in shame. Although he wanted to believe that his brother was going straight, hearing this news, it certainly wasn't something that was unbelievable. Though he didn't want to think that his brother would kidnap and harm children, he couldn't put it past him either.

"I, uh, I didn't know."

Jacobs continued to watch him for a minute and read his body language. Wickerson didn't seem like a guy who was trying to sell him a bill of goods. He appeared to be choking up and getting upset over the news, sounding like it was something he wasn't previously aware of.

"OK, taking you at your word that you don't know anything about it, maybe you can help me find these kids," Jacobs said.

Wickerson threw his hands up, not having any idea how to help. "How? I couldn't tell you where he's at."

"I've heard that he's gone somewhere that he hasn't been before. That crosses off any places Mallette's associated with. Where else would he go?"

Wickerson shook his head, honestly having no idea. "I really don't know. He never mentioned anything else."

"You're sure?"

"Yes."

"If I don't get to these kids soon, there's a good chance they might be dead," Jacobs said. "You really want that on your conscience?"

"No, of course not, but I don't know how to help you. I don't know where he is."

Jacobs wasn't ready to give up yet, not necessarily because he knew Wickerson knew more than he was telling, but more so out of desperation, hoping there was something that he thought was trivial would come rushing back to him. Something that would be crucial to finding Wickers. "Think back to your conversation. Replay everything in your mind. Everything that was said. There's gotta be something else you guys talked about. It couldn't have just been about renting the building."

"I mean, yeah, we talked about some stuff, but nothing..." Wickerson said, sighing, trying to replay the conversation in his mind.

"Other names, other places, dates, anything that

might not seem important at first glance that might indicate where I can find him. Even if it's just another lead to check out."

Wickerson continued thinking for a minute, shaking his head, nothing coming to him. He spit out a few things, but nothing that indicated much of anything. Then, something struck him. "Wait a minute."

"You got something?"

"Umm, I dunno. The one time we were talking, and we were just kind of rambling, and since I thought he was going straight, I asked him if he had a girlfriend or anything."

"What'd he say?"

"He said he was seeing a girl named Amber."

"Get a last name?" Jacobs asked.

Wickerson shook his head. "No, we didn't get that involved in it. He just said it in passing and that was it."

Jacobs then thought about using Wickerson, just as he did with Wiggins, to get to Wickers. He was willing to deal with just about anybody to get a beat on where Wickers was now. But the same thing applied as to whether Jacobs could truly trust him. Though he thought Wickerson had been truthful and genuine up to now, he knew even from his time on the police force that when push came to shove, no matter what the circumstances, sometimes family members just wouldn't give up one another no matter how bad things were. But just as he did with Wiggins, it was a shot worth taking.

"If you called him now and talked to him, you think you could get him to reveal where he's at?" Jacobs asked.

Wickerson wasn't sure it was something he wanted to do and took a few seconds to think about it before responding. "I don't know. I wouldn't know what to say."

"Just gotta try and get him to reveal where he's at. Or even a clue of where he's at. There's three kids' lives at stake here."

Wickerson nodded, acknowledging he realized the seriousness of the situation, even though he was nervous about getting further involved. "Yeah. Yeah, I'll call him." Wickerson reached into his pocket and pulled out his phone. He stared at it for a second before looking for his brother's number. Once he scrolled to it, he looked at Jacobs before finally dialing. "Should I mention you?"

"Not a good idea," Jacobs answered.

As Wickerson put the phone to his ear, Jacobs wasn't getting his hopes up or expecting much. He assumed that Wickers wouldn't give much information, and the thought occurred to him that the man wouldn't even answer the phone. Jacobs was pleasantly surprised, though, when Wickerson started talking. Wickers did pick up, just as the phone was about to go to voicemail.

"Hey, just wanted to see how you were doing?" Wickerson said.

"I'm all right," Wickers replied. "I really can't talk right now. I'll give you a call back later."

"No, wait, there's something I really gotta talk to you about. It's important."

"What is it?"

"The police were just here a few minutes ago asking about you."

"Oh? What for?"

"It was in connection to that building that I rented for you. They said they found some dead bodies in there and wanted to know if I knew where you were."

"I didn't have anything to do with that."

"What the hell's going on?" Wickerson asked. "You told me you were starting a business and now I got police looking at me in connection with some stuff that you're doing. I'm not going to jail for whatever you're doing. That building's in my name, Johnny."

"I know that, I know that. I'll figure something out, trust me. I'll get you out of this."

"Trust you? I wouldn't even be in this situation if it wasn't for you."

"Just... trust me. I'll figure something out," Wickers said, talking louder to drown out the noise of a plane passing over him. He waited for a few seconds until the noise was gone so he could talk in his normal voice. "You're not in custody or nothing, are you?"

"No, they just came here to talk. They left a few

minutes ago. But they were talking to me like they thought I was involved in whatever happened there."

"I'll figure out a way to straighten everything out. You got my word on that."

"Well, where are you right now? Because they told me they're looking for you."

"Don't worry about that. I'm not anywhere they can find me."

"You're gonna leave me hanging for this, aren't you?"

"No, I told you I'm gonna take care of this and I will. Believe me, they won't hang this on you."

"Well, how are you gonna take care of this?" Wickerson asked.

"I'll handle it."

"Should I come over to you?"

"No, no, just stay put for now."

"You with that girl of yours, Amber? Because they said they thought you two might be together."

"How they know about her?"

"Beats me."

"No, she ain't here. She's out of town for a couple days."

"Well, if you're in her house, they might be showing up there. Might wanna think about moving."

"Nah, I'm not in a house."

"Johnny?"

"Yeah?"

"They also said something about you having a couple of kids with you," Wickerson said.

"Listen, I gotta get going."

"Johnny, what are you doing? How'd it get to this?"

"I'm just doing what I gotta do," Wickers answered.

"Kids, John? Kids?"

"I don't need any lectures from you. You know I'm tired of hearing all that. That's why I left before. Been hearing lectures my whole life from Dad and you about what I'm doing or not doing. I don't wanna hear it no more."

Wickers hung up, not wanting to hear anything else or continue the conversation any longer.

"Johnny? Johnny?" Wickerson said, feeling like he failed. He looked up at Jacobs and shook his head, wishing he could have gotten more. "He's gone."

"Anything?"

"Just that his girl's out of town and that he's not at her house."

"What about background noises? Something you heard... strange sound, voices, anything like that?"

Wickerson thought back, hoping something would pop out at him. Nothing did initially. "Wait. I did hear something."

"What was it?"

"A plane. It sounded really close like he had to speak up over it to be heard at one point."

"Close to the airport," Jacobs said.

Wickerson let out a deep sigh, nothing else coming

to him. "That's it. That's all there was. No other noises or sounds that I can recall."

"It's OK. It's a good start."

"So, what now?"

"Now I go find him before he does something really stupid."

"What about those bodies?" Wickerson asked. "Am I gonna get into trouble for that?"

"When the police come knocking, just tell them the truth. And leave the part about me being here out."

"Why?"

"Me and the police are on the same side, but I operate a little differently than they do. They wouldn't like my methods. And right now, my only priority is saving those kids before it's too late."

Wickerson nodded in agreement, not even taking a second to think about it.

"Sorry about that bump on your head," Jacobs said. "Wasn't sure which side you were on."

Wickerson dabbed at the back of his head to make sure it wasn't bleeding, which it wasn't. "Forget it. Probably what I deserved for letting that idiot take advantage of me. Consider it a hard lesson learned for me."

The two shook hands, and then Jacobs left. As he started driving, he called Franks to let him know the latest developments and explained the conversation the two brothers had.

"By the airport?" Franks asked.

"Sure sounds like it."

"Airport's a big place, man."

"I know it."

"I mean, he could be anywhere around there."

"I know that," Jacobs said. "Can you get Hack started on searching around the airport?"

"Yeah, I guess. But why knock yourself out trying to figure this out? I mean, they're gonna call you and tell you where they wanna meet anyway. Why not just wait for that call and prepare for that?"

"Because those kids shouldn't be in his clutches for one second longer than they already are."

"Yeah, you're right about that."

"Plus, whenever they call, they'll be waiting for me. I'll have the advantage if I can turn the tables and surprise them. And if there's one thing I like… it's a surprise party."

## 14

By the time Jacobs got back to the pawn shop, Hack was already hard at work trying to find where Wickers was hiding by the airport.

"Come up with anything?" Jacobs asked as soon as he entered the office.

"Working on it," Hack replied, typing away.

"Well, let's think about it. If he had to find another place quickly, we can probably eliminate a bunch of places off the top."

"Unless he had a second place all along," Franks said. "Maybe he planned for something like this in case something went wrong at the antique store."

"But why use your brother and get him involved, and possibly be a loose end, if you're already planning on a backup? Why go through all that hassle? All that's doing is creating another problem. If you're already counting on a second place, you can make the first place almost anywhere, doesn't matter if I know where it is or not, right?"

Franks shrugged. "I guess so."

"Well, let's go under the assumption right now that he had to find another place quickly," Jacobs said. "Where would he go near the airport?"

"If he's working on short notice, I'd say a hotel or something. Not enough time to rent a house or building."

"Hack?"

"I was just trying to track down his cell phone signal," he replied. "I can confirm it was by the airport but I can't get a read on exactly where. He also hasn't used any credit cards or anything that can be traced back to him."

"I dunno, does anyone else get the feeling they wouldn't pick a hotel?" Jacobs asked. "Seems kind of high profile for something like this, don't you think?"

"Seems like an odd choice," Franks said. "Seems like it'd be too close in there. Not enough room to spread out. Unless they figure that's the best way to keep you in their sights."

"Yeah, but if there's gunplay, in a hotel, police will be there within minutes. Doesn't seem like the smarter option considering they might not get out before the cops get there."

"Who said they were smart?"

"Smart enough to get this far."

"What about Mallette? Does he have any property in the area? Business, residence, anything?"

Jacobs' facial expression indicated he thought it was entirely possible. "That's a good idea. If things go bad with your first option, especially when you've tried something different, what do you do? Retreat back to someplace familiar."

Jacobs and Franks looked to Hack to have him start checking, but he was already listening and well ahead of them. "I'm on it," he said, not having to be told.

"You know, maybe we should check on the girl-friend," Franks said. "Just to be sure that she is out of town. Never know, maybe Wickers was just saying that to throw anyone off the track. He's not exactly what I'd call a trustworthy source."

"That's a good idea," Jacobs said. "Because that would be my first choice as far as where to look."

"Even if she is out of town, doesn't mean they're not using her place."

Jacobs rushed out of the office, not wanting to stay in there for another minute.

"Where you going?" Franks asked.

"Gonna check out her place. No use sitting around here doing nothing. Might as well see for sure. Text me her address."

Franks sat down on one of the computers that Hack had set up and started looking for the address of Wickers' girlfriend. "That dude's like a one-man task force."

"I certainly would never want to be on his bad side," Hack replied.

"I don't know if being on his good side's much better," Franks said, drawing a laugh.

It took Jacobs about twenty minutes to reach the girlfriend's apartment. Since her apartment was on the third floor, he really couldn't stake out the building to find out whether she was actually there or not. There was only one thing he could do... knock and find out. He immediately went up to the third floor and marched to her apartment, knocking on the door. After a few minutes of non-activity, Jacobs was starting to believe that Amber really was out of town. As he stood there debating what to do, another man came walking down the hallway.

"You looking for Amber?" the man asked.

"Yeah. You know where she is?"

"Out of town. Must've left two or three days ago. Said she'd be gone about a week, so she'll probably be back in a few days."

"Oh. Thanks. Appreciate the help."

"No problem, bud."

As the man disappeared from sight, Jacobs started walking down the hall to leave. He had thoughts about staying and trying to get into the apartment to see if there were any clues as to where Wickers might be, but wasn't sure if he should. Finally, he decided he would and walked back to the apartment. He took a look around to make sure nobody else was coming along and seeing what he was doing and quickly jimmied open the door. He didn't want to completely dismantle the door and have anybody who was walking by see that somebody had broken in. Jacobs wasn't planning on destroying the place and hoped to leave everything just the way he found it.

Once inside, he put on a pair of leather gloves to make sure he didn't leave any prints behind, just in case something happened to the woman and police wound up dusting the place for fingerprints. He knew it was just his paranoia, but he thought it better to be safe than sorry. He first searched the living room, going through the couches and furniture, closets, and table drawers. He then moved to the kitchen, going through all the cabinets. After that, he searched the bathroom, then the bedroom, checking under the bed, the closet, and all the dresser drawers. He turned the place inside out, though not messily so, and thoroughly checked everything twice. He was there for a good thirty minutes making sure he didn't miss anything. Unfortunately, it was all for naught as he didn't find a single thing that pointed to Wickers at all. In fact, there wasn't even anything in the apartment that indicated she knew him in the slightest.

Jacobs left the apartment and stood in the hallway looking around as he closed the door. With no one there, he slunk down the hall and exited the building. Once he got back to his car, he sat in it and stared out the window before turning it on. He called Franks to let him know he came up empty.

"So, you didn't get anything?" Franks asked.

"Not a thing. She's either one of the most meticulous people there is, or she doesn't know much about what Wickers does for a living."

"Or he coached her up and told her not to have any incriminating evidence around."

"I dunno. Doesn't really matter in either case," Jacobs said.

"You still there?"

"No, I left already. Just sitting here in the parking lot thinking."

Hack started snapping his fingers, interrupting Franks as he was about to say something insightful. Franks was a little startled and turned to face him as he wondered what he was doing.

"You got some ants in your pants or something?" Franks asked.

Hack looked at him with a face like he couldn't believe that was the response he had. "Really? I'm pretty sure that expression went out with the third grade."

"Well, maybe some of us still like to talk like we're on a third-grade level. Ever think of that?"

"Unfortunately, the thought has crossed my mind."

Franks grinned but was eager to get on with it, knowing he must have found something important. "Hold on, Brett, the boy genius might have something."

"Boy genius?" Hack said, not endeared to the term.

"Don't get your panties in a twist. Whatcha got?" Franks walked over to him and put his arm around his shoulder as he leaned in to view the computer.

Hack pointed to the screen so Franks could easily see what he was talking about. "See this here?"

"A used car lot?"

"Yeah."

"So? What about it?"

"This lot has come up about four times in the various searches that I've been looking into," Hack said.

"OK? So, what's the connection?"

"Well, on the surface there isn't one."

"On the surface?" Franks asked. "How about below the surface?"

"Well, below the surface, the business is owned by a company called BER Limited."

"Which is interesting because? Hold up, before you start answering this, let me tell Brett to come back here so I don't have him on hold all day."

"That'd be nice," Jacobs said.

"Oh. Guess you heard, huh?"

"Yeah. Neither of you guys talk softly."

"Well, get back here on the double while we go over this," Franks said. "Hopefully we'll have it figured out by the time you get back here."

Jacobs agreed to come right back as the two of them tried to decipher what Hack had come up with.

"Anyway, so let's get back to the game here," Franks said.

"I forget where I was."

"BER Limited."

"Oh, yeah," Hack said. "So, this company has come up a few times in my search. At first I kind of just shrugged it off, figuring it was some overseas company that Mallette did business with to try and legitimize his businesses."

"But you don't think so?"

"No, I think Mallette owns BER Limited. Or, I should say he's at least got a stake in it. It seems to be owned by a couple guys, all of whom can be connected or traced back to him. All but one guy that is. And I can't find anything on him."

"YOU can't find anything on him? That's saying a lot."

"I can't find anything on him because I don't think he exists."

"How can that be?" Franks asked.

"I think it's an alias that Rich Mallette uses. Or has used in the past."

Franks leaned in even further, studying the information on the screen. Though it seemed to make sense, he still wasn't seeing how it connected to their current situation. "Yeah, OK, I guess I can see where you're going with that. But how does it fit in with Wickers?"

Hack looked at him for a second before answering. "Because this car lot is on the outskirts of the airport."

Franks didn't immediately respond, taking it all in. "So, you're thinking that Wickers went there?"

Hack nodded. "I think it's a good possibility. Think about it. We know he went near the airport somewhere. It's not likely he went to a public place. He probably went somewhere he's familiar with. A place that Mallette has ties to that he's probably been to before at one time or another."

"Could be."

They continued conversing for a little while, discussing the merits of whether Wickers would actually be in the auto lot. Hack tried digging further into it and found that the lot was still an active business. That made things a little more challenging, as well as murkier. They'd always assumed that if Wickers took up shop in another business, like the warehouse, or the antique shop, that it wouldn't be doing active day-to-day business. But this place seemed like it was. Had its own website which seemed up to date, along with photos from the internet and recent reviews that indicated it was indeed very much active.

By the time Jacobs arrived, they'd already dug up a good bit of information on the business. He hadn't really been told anything yet, though he knew they must have found something interesting by the way Franks put him on hold earlier, then had him come straight back. Jacobs just hoped it wasn't another dead end.

"So, what do you guys got?" Jacobs asked as soon as he entered the office.

Franks let Hack do the explaining since he was the one who found it. After Hack finished, Jacobs agreed that it was likely a Mallette company, though he didn't know it for sure.

"We've always known that Mallette's done business outside of his own name," Jacobs said. "But it was never something that we could prove as illegal. The other businesses that is. We thought he used most of them as fronts to mask his other illegal activities, but there was always a prevailing notion that he had a few that were strictly legit, just to cover his tracks. That way in case there were doubts about him, he could point to the legal businesses to throw some doubt on whether he was operating the illegal ones."

"Did you actually pinpoint specific businesses?" Franks asked.

"Yeah. Some of them, anyway. But we knew he had a hand in a lot more than we could prove or even suspect."

"What do you think about this auto one?" Hack asked.

"Could be it," Jacobs answered. "I mean, it fits."

"But it's an active business with people coming in and out," Franks said. "Don't you think that's kind of a risky place to bring some kids to?"

Jacobs acknowledged the issues with it, but also knew it was still possible. "How big is this place?"

Hack pulled up pictures online and showed him. It was a fairly big place. It wasn't just some small trailer on a tiny lot selling a few cars a month. This was a lot that had several offices and buildings, a repair garage, and seemed to do a good bit of business.

"Could be that they have a designated place that they do business in," Jacobs said. "Maybe an office or garage that's off to the side or something that Mallette's kept off limits for the people who work there."

"You think everyone who works there might be involved?" Franks asked.

"Nah, I doubt it. They might know one of the owners is into some shady stuff, maybe even noticed a strange thing here or there, but I doubt most of them, if any, are actually involved themselves in anything. I'd be surprised if they were."

"So, assuming that this is in fact the place and the kids, along with Wickers, are there, how you gonna do this? You can't just go in there guns a blazing with ten or twenty people working there along with any customers. That just ain't gonna fly."

Jacobs knew he was right. Going into a crowded business with people all around was a surefire way of getting a lot of innocent people hurt. Not to mention the fact that the police would probably get there long before he was able to get out since he'd have to maneuver around so many people.

"Well, what time does this place close?" Jacobs asked.

"Looks like eight o'clock," Hack replied.

"So, they're obviously planning on doing the exchange later at night, right?"

"That's the theory," Franks answered.

"Well, if this place closes at eight, figure everyone should be out by nine?"

"Probably."

"Say they call me at nine to meet there at ten," Jacobs said, trying to talk things through in his own mind. "If I get there early and am already there when I get the call, then I can still get the jump on them."

"You hit them almost immediately after the call, like minutes, it might work. They definitely wouldn't be expecting it," Hack said.

As what seemed to be the usual, Franks had to be the one to put a damper on things. "I, uh, hate to be the one to always be disagreeing here and pointing out the bad things that can happen."

"But?" Jacobs said.

"But, there's one small issue with that. OK, maybe it's a big issue."

"Which is?"

"You don't know for sure that they're there. It's OK to have a gut feeling, but what if you get there, they call you, and you find out the meeting place is clear across the other side of town?"

"Then I guess I'll have a problem."

## 15

Jacobs got to the car dealership around seven o'clock and waited in his car across the street. He kept his eyes glued to the business, hoping to see someone he'd recognize, such as one of Mallette's Maulers. Part of him thought of going into the dealership and walking around, but he thought it might be too chancy. If even one person recognized him, it was likely to blow the entire plan sky high. Once they saw he was there, they'd hightail it in minutes and he'd have to start all over again. No, he had to stick to his plan, even though it was difficult for him to stay patient. He kept in touch with Franks periodically, to let him know he was there, and let him know if he saw anything unusual.

At eight o'clock, he saw the employees start closing up shop. They put gates down near the entrance and exits. Gunner was in the passenger seat, starting to move around. Jacobs could sense he was getting restless. He put his hand on the dog's head and started rubbing it.

"I know, bud, I feel it too."

Jacobs continued watching, seeing car upon car leave the lot. He was starting to get anxious, wondering when the phone call was going to come. It had to be soon, he thought. After a bunch of cars left, there was no activity for a while. Jacobs got the feeling that all the employees had now left. Every now and then, his eyes drifted toward his phone to look at the time, while also hoping that it would ring. At nine o'clock on the dot, he finally got his wish. He quickly and eagerly snapped it up, not even letting the first ring finish.

"Yeah?"

"I guess I should give you props for what you did at the antique shop earlier," Wickers said.

"No different than what I'm gonna do to you."

Wickers laughed. "Such confidence."

"Well, you obviously don't have any or you wouldn't have left. What's the matter? Too scared to face me?"

"I'm all about playing the odds."

"The odds are unless you release those kids, I'm gonna kick your ass."

"Well, that's what this call's about, right? You show up unarmed to the place that I tell you, and once we see you, we'll let the kids go."

"Not gonna happen."

"Then these kids are dead."

"I'll show up to wherever you tell me, but it won't be unarmed. I know how you operate. I'll come in unarmed, you shoot me, then kill them. I'm not gonna play that game."

"Then I guess we don't have anything to talk about," Wickers said.

"I'll come in. I'll give myself up. With guns in my hand. Once you release the kids, I'll send them somewhere, and I'll stay behind. I'll drop my guns when they're safely out of sight."

"How do I know I can trust that you'll do that? What makes me believe that you won't start shooting once the kids are gone?"

"Same way I know I can trust you," Jacobs said.

Wickers thought it over for a minute. He still wasn't totally sure that he could trust that Jacobs would fulfill his part of the bargain, but he figured it really didn't matter. As soon as Jacobs got within their sights, they were going to kill him. They still had four men against just him. Even if Jacobs did something funny, Wickers was sure they could handle it since they had the numbers.

"Fine," Wickers finally agreed.

"Where and when?"

"There's a used car dealership by the airport called First Class Auto Sales."

Jacobs' eyes immediately looked up to the sign in

front of the lot that had the same name. "Not sure exactly where it's at, but I'm sure I'll find it."

"I'm sure you will."

"What time?"

"One hour from now," Wickers said. "Don't be late. We'll wait for ten minutes. If you're not here ten minutes after ten o'clock, we're gone, and trust me, the kids will be too. We won't try again."

"I'll be there."

"And one more thing: if we see any police cars, or even get the slightest sniff of one, or we think there's anyone else out there besides you, you can kiss these kids goodbye. You understand?"

"I understand. How am I gonna get into this dealership? Is there a gate or doors or something I have to get through?" Jacobs asked.

"I'll have a man at the gate to let you in. He'll lead you up to where you need to go. And just so you don't get any funny ideas, he'll have a radio on him to check in. If you decide you're gonna try and lessen the odds and take him out before you get here, I wouldn't do it. I'm gonna call him before you get to where you need to go, and if he doesn't answer because he's dead, those kids will be too."

"No funny business."

"See you in an hour."

Jacobs put the phone down and looked at Gunner. "Time to go to work." He gave the dog a few pats on the head before picking up his phone again. He wanted to let Franks know what was going on.

"Hear anything?" Franks asked.

"It's going down. One hour. Right here at the auto dealership."

"Awesome. What's the deal? What do you need? Anything?"

"Yeah, I could use you down here to take the kids," Jacobs said.

"Why?"

"I just wanna make sure I take all the right precautions in making sure those kids get home. If I have to sacrifice myself for them to get away, or stay behind, I wanna make sure there's someone else here who can get them out of here."

Franks really didn't like hearing him talk like that, but understood his reasoning. "So, what do you need me to do?"

"If you can come down here, park across the street, facing the lot. If I get in any trouble and can't make it back with them, I'll tell them to keep following the path to the main gate. If you see them, you grab them and get them out quickly."

"And you?"

"Don't look back."

Franks sighed, but knew it was for the best. "Yeah, yeah, I'll be there. What time?"

"I'm gonna move in a few minutes to try and get the jump on them so get here as soon as you can."

"All right, I'll be there in about thirty minutes."

Jacobs looked at the time. "Thirty minutes it is. Just make sure you're not late. Those kids might not have time to wait on you."

"Hey, I will be there. No need to worry about that."

"Good. Thanks."

"Good luck," Franks said.

"Yeah."

Figuring whatever was about to go down, it would happen quick. So Jacobs waited another five minutes in his car before doing anything. He didn't want to go in too fast, then wind up having the kids standing there before Franks was able to get there in the event he was too busy holding Wickers and the others off. But he also couldn't wait too long considering he still didn't know where the kids were being held. Since the dealership only sold used cars, it wasn't as big as some of the new car dealerships, but he still wanted to give him enough time where he could figure out the best way to go.

After five minutes, Jacobs got out of the car, holding Gunner on a leash, even though the dog was pretty good at not wandering off if he didn't have one on. After a couple cars went by, they crossed the street and ducked under the single bar that gate system that adorned the exit. They immediately ran to the first building they came across and clung to it to avoid being spotted in the open. Jacobs didn't want to be in front so he went to the back of the building. As he turned the corner he saw the building had some bay doors, indicating to him that it was the repair garage. He kept going until he came to another building with some large windows. He figured it was the showroom and office spaces. Everything was dark so he couldn't tell if anyone was in there, but assumed he'd see some type of light to indicate it was occupied if they were there.

Jacobs kept moving until he got to the edge of the building. There were several more buildings across from it, though he couldn't tell if any of them were in use at the moment. The lot actually wasn't as big as Jacobs thought it was. He wondered how Wickers would be able to hide out there all afternoon without bumping into people. He just waited there for a few more minutes, hoping he'd see or hear some movement that would tip off where the men were. But there was nothing.

After a few more minutes, Jacobs thought he heard a car coming. He saw headlights shining on one of the buildings he hadn't checked yet, then heard the engine roar a little louder as it came closer. Jacobs knelt as Gunner sat next to him. He peeked around the corner of the building as the car finally stopped in front of what appeared to be a maintenance facility, about half the car in Jacobs' line of sight. All four doors opened up with men exiting the car and approaching the door of the building. Then Jacobs saw the little legs of children going by and he knew it was them. Wickers must have called from a nearby area, waiting for all the workers to leave before coming over himself. After they all went in, Jacobs noticed a light go on.

He looked at the time and saw they still had about thirty minutes to go. Jacobs knew he still had the upper hand and could proceed at his pace. He knew he had both the element of surprise and the luxury of knowing what Wickers had planned. Jacobs knew at some point one of them was going to go down to the front gate when they expected him to arrive. That cut down the immediate threat to three. Unless he decided to take that guy out first, then take care of the others, that way he wouldn't have to worry about him coming back up behind him. But he also knew that Franks would be arriving soon, probably in about five minutes. In the end, Jacobs thought it was best to cut the odds down by one and wait until one of them left the building to go to the front gate. He sent Franks a quick text message to let him know what he was doing that way he wouldn't be worrying about not seeing anybody yet. Franks immediately replied to let him know he'd wait. Franks figured he'd hear gunshots first, anyway.

Jacobs took another minute to decide where he'd attack first. He thought it'd be best to wait until one of them came down to the gate and take him out first. That way there'd only be three left, and if he had to stay behind while the kids got away, he didn't have to worry about them running into him. This way, he knew as long as he got them out of that building, they'd make it to safety. The only problem was that he didn't know how long it would be until someone came out. They might take it all the way up to the meeting time, which meant Jacobs wouldn't get as big of a surprise as he'd like. But he figured he'd still be able to get the jump on them since they wouldn't expect him to come up alone.

Jacobs waited another ten minutes before he saw any other movement. The door to the maintenance facility opened and a man stepped out. Jacobs hoped this was it. The man closed the door and then started walking down to the front gate. Jacobs stayed behind for a minute just to make sure nobody else was coming out, in case they had some plan in place to have a second pair of eyes out there. It didn't seem they did, though. With his mind made up, he scurried back behind the buildings again until he got to the front. He peeked around the corner and saw the man standing by the gate, smoking a cigarette. Right now the man was facing him, though not looking in his direction, but still, it'd be hard for Jacobs to come up on him. Jacobs could easily take him out with a bullet, but the shot would definitely be heard by the others, thereby ending his element of surprise. His best bet was to get in close and take him out without making a sound. Jacobs was going to have to get behind him somehow.

As Jacobs thought of how to take care of the man, he looked down at Gunner. He could use the dog as a distraction. He just had to hope that Gunner didn't go too far. But Jacobs had confidence in the dog that their training would keep working just as it had up to that point. Jacobs got down to a knee and released his hand from the leash. He then pointed to the man by the gate.

"Gunner, easy," Jacobs said, which was his command for the dog to just loiter by a target or situation without being aggressive.

Up to now, in training exercises, Gunner properly complied with the command about ninety percent of the time. The times when Gunner didn't do the right thing, it was because he usually came right back to Jacobs without staying near the target. Jacobs usually used a dummy for the training, though both Franks and Hack had also volunteered their services a few times as well. Gunner got about halfway up the building, still not yet in the clear, and stopped. Jacobs sighed, thinking the dog was about to turn around and come back to him. Gunner turned his head around and looked at his owner, who tried to spur him on by motioning and pointing to the other man. Gunner turned his head back around and continued on with his mission. As he cleared the building, Jacobs started moving into place as well. He clung to the side of the building, using the cloak of darkness to his advantage.

"Hey little guy, what are you doing around here?" the man said, petting Gunner as he stood near his legs.

As Gunner accepted the guy petting him, he was turning the man around at the same time. The first sign of the man turning his back to Jacobs, he wasted no time in moving. Jacobs sprang off the wall and ran full speed towards the man, jumping on his back and putting his arm around the man's neck. Jacobs buried his forearm into the man's throat as the man desperately tried to get out of the choke hold. As they struggled, they eventually fell backwards, landing squarely on Jacobs' back, though he never relinquished the hold. The man flailed away, trying to move Jacobs' arm off of his neck. Jacobs squeezed even harder, ending the man's dire predicament. Once Jacobs felt the man's body go limp, he finally let go. He pushed the man off him as Jacobs immediately looked back to make sure nobody else was coming.

Remembering that the man had a radio on him, Jacobs went back to his body and started looking for it. He thought it might come in handy if they said something that might help his planning. He padded down the man's pockets but didn't find anything. Then he noticed the radio was lying a few feet away, assuming that it dropped from the man's belt when Jacobs attacked him. Jacobs picked it up, then he and Gunner went back behind the buildings again until they came within view of the maintenance facility. Jacobs looked at the time and saw that there was ten minutes to go. He had to move now or else he thought he'd lose the surprise factor. Then they'd be waiting for him. He quickly devised a plan that he hoped would work, though he wasn't sure. Jacobs took a quick look at

Gunner. Then he grabbed the radio and started speaking in it.

"Need help down here now!" Jacobs yelled, trying to disguise his voice, even though he had no idea what the other man sounded like. All he wanted to do was try and make it sound like not his own and to convey a sense of panic.

"What's going on?" a voice replied.

"Help!"

Jacobs didn't want to give them too much. He wanted to make them wonder what was going on, and since it was before he was supposed to get there, hopefully, confuse them as to what was going on. He hoped that another one would come out to check what was going on, and make them think if it was something else other than him, and get it cleared up before he was supposed to get there. The plan seemed to work as the door opened up again. A man came out and stood there for a moment, trying to see if anything was happening. From his vantage point, though, it wasn't a good angle to the front of the property and he couldn't see or hear anything.

The man turned back around and yelled inside to the others. "I'll take a walk down there and see what's going on."

"Radio back and let us know what's happening," Wickers replied.

The man closed the door and started heading for the front gate. Now was the time to cut their numbers in half. But Jacobs still didn't want to shoot and give himself away yet. He figured he'd let the dog continue his training.

"Gunner, get him!"

Gunner immediately took off like a rocket and ran full force after the man. By the time the man heard him coming, he turned around just in time to see the German Shepherd lunging at him, grabbing him by the arm and sinking his teeth into his skin. As he was doing that, Jacobs ran towards the door of the building, setting himself up on the other side of it, waiting for it to open again. Now, he was hoping the men left inside would hear some commotion going on outside and would come out to investigate. As the man was being attacked by Gunner, and trying to fend himself off, he was making a loud enough noise to alert the men inside. He was screaming and hollering, but still no one came out yet. Jacobs got another idea to help that process along.

"Someone help get this dog off me!" Jacobs radioed.

"What the hell's going on?" Wickers replied.

A few seconds later the door opened again. Another man emerged and took a few steps outside, seeing the commotion with the dog as they were plainly in view not too far ahead of him. The man let out a small laugh, somehow seeing humor in it, then took a few more steps to take care of it.

"Hold on, hold on, I'm coming," the man said.

As soon as the door closed behind him, Jacobs sprang into action. He put his arm around the man's neck, grabbing hold of it, and jamming his gun into the man's side. Before the man even had any chance to resist, Jacobs unloaded three rounds into the man's side, killing him instantly. Jacobs took his arm off the man's throat as the man slid down to the ground. With that man taken care of, Jacobs immediately looked to Gunner, who still had his teeth into his man's arm. The man was trying with his free arm to push the dog off him but wasn't having any luck. Gunner was dug in deep and not letting go until recalled. But Jacobs thought Gunner had done his job long enough, and he didn't want to wait any longer and risk him getting hurt if the man was able to pull out a gun on him. By now, Wickers was inside and knew he was here. It didn't matter about keeping inconspicuous any longer.

"Gunner, release!"

Almost immediately after hearing the command, Gunner did what was requested of him and let go of the man's arm. After letting go, he started running back to Jacobs' position. With a clear shot now, Jacobs pumped several more rounds into the man's stomach and chest, killing him by the time he fell over onto his back. With Gunner now back by his side, Jacobs leaned up against the side of the building again, taking a few deep breaths to calm himself before he went any further.

Jacobs put his hand on the door and quickly

yanked it open. He didn't yet make himself visible or go through it in the event Wickers was waiting for him and took a shot. Jacobs didn't want to make himself an easy target.

"Gunner, seek."

Gunner sprinted through the door and almost immediately started growling. Jacobs took a peek around the door and saw Gunner standing there, still growling. Jacobs got down low, almost crawling through the door. Only a few feet away was Gunner. He was in front of the kids, who were sitting down in chairs, tied to them. Tucked away behind them was Wickers, trying to use them as a shield. Only his face and his gun were visible as he pointed his weapon between two of the children at Jacobs.

"You got nowhere to go," Jacobs said, pointing his own weapon at his target. "Your friends are gone, they can't help you. And nobody else is coming."

"Only thing I need is sitting right in front of me."

"You do something to them and there's nothing in the world that can save you. There'll be nothing between you and me to stop me."

"But you won't take any chances right now, will you?" Wickers asked. "Never know which way a gun will go or if a finger will slip on the trigger. Bullet could go just about anywhere."

"Don't be stupid. There's no way out of this for you."

"Well, if that's the case, maybe I should just take

everyone with me." Gunner started growling again, causing Wickers to worry that he was close to attacking. "Same could be said for that dog. He can be the first one to go."

"Assuming you can get to him before he does to you."

Although he was itching to blow a hole through Wickers' body, Jacobs had to be cautious. There was nothing more important than the safety of the kids sitting in front of him. And he could tell they were scared out of their minds.

"I'll tell you what I'll do," Jacobs said, hoping to end the standoff as peacefully as possible. "Let them go with me right now, and I'll let you leave here. Can't guarantee you'll live through tomorrow, but for today, you'll get another day."

"I could say the same to you. Let me leave right now and I'll guarantee their safety another day."

Jacobs shook his head. "Not gonna happen. I'm not letting these kids out of my sight again. Besides, you're fresh out of options."

"How you figure?" Wickers asked.

"Shots have been fired. Police have probably been notified and are on the way. What do you think they're gonna do when they find you in here with a gun and three kids tied up in a chair?"

"You're just guessing. You don't know they're on the way."

"And you don't know they're not."

"Even if they are, so what? You're in here with a gun too."

"I'm a former cop. Still got friends on the force. I tell them the story of you kidnapping three of my relatives and all those bodies out front was me defending myself and my family... with the history I have with Mallette... who you think they're gonna believe?"

Sweat was pouring off Wickers' face as he knew Jacobs was right and had the upper hand. If he stayed as he was, there was a chance he'd be going to jail. Let the kids go and move and there was a chance he'd end up dead. Either way, it wasn't much of a choice for him. Going to jail was almost like being dead in his eyes. He had to make a decision and make it quick. He did what he thought would at least give him a chance. Wickers stood up, though he still kept his gun pointed at the back of one of the boys' head. He then took a couple steps back.

"Fine. You let me walk out the back door and they're all yours."

"Hurry it up," Jacobs said, anxious for the ordeal to be over with.

Wickers continued making his way to the back door, backing up slowly, still with his gun pointed at the children in case Jacobs reneged on the deal. "Just don't shoot."

As Wickers backed up, without the protection of the kids, Jacobs knew he could have drilled him easily. But he thought the children had been through enough.

They didn't need to see someone getting killed right in front of them. Plus, Wickers was right about one thing, there was no telling where bullets might fly after the shooting started. If Wickers' finger pulled the trigger as a reflex action after getting shot and one of the bullets hit the kids, Jacobs would always question his decision. As Wickers got near the back door, Gunner started growling again. Wickers pointed his gun at the dog, fearing he might charge.

"Gunner, easy."

Gunner looked at his owner and stopped growling. Wickers finally reached the door, then pushed it open with his free hand. "No hard feelings." Wickers then raced through the door and into the night, hoping he'd get a chance at Jacobs another day.

With Wickers gone, Jacobs quickly rushed over to the kids and untied them from their chairs.

"You guys OK?" Jacobs asked, getting a hug from all of them.

"We're fine," the girl said. "We're just scared and wanna see Mom and Dad."

"OK, now listen, there's a car down at the front gate that's gonna take you out of here. Just go down the path and there's a guy there waiting. I know the guy, you can trust him."

"But what about you?"

"I have to go after that guy to make sure he never comes after you again. OK?"

"What if there's someone else out there?"

"There's not. I promise. Gunner will go with you," Jacobs said, pointing to the dog. "He'll protect you."

The girl didn't seem too sure about the idea, but agreed.

"I'll see you soon."

The kids followed Jacobs out the front door, with him staying in front of them to protect them just in case Wickers decided to double back.

"Go," Jacobs said. The kids started running down the path to the front gate. "Gunner, protect." Gunner just stood there for a second, not complying with the command. "Gunner, protect." Hearing it a second time, Gunner finally complied and raced down the path with the kids, staying at their side. Jacobs stood there for a few seconds to make sure there were no issues, then raced around the back of the building to start looking for Wickers.

As soon as the kids were in view of the gate, Franks pushed down on the pedal and zoomed out of the parking lot, tires squealing as he sped to the front of the property. The kids looked around for a second, not seeing anyone waiting for them. They were starting to get worried. Then Franks raced in front of them and got out to open the back door.

"C'mon kids, I'm with your uncle Brett," Franks said. "I'll take you to your parents." The kids quickly hopped into the car. As they did, Gunner stood by the gate, watching them. "Gunner, in." But Gunner wasn't taking commands from anyone other than Jacobs on this night.

"What about the dog?" one of the boys asked.

"Gunner, in," Franks repeated.

Gunner looked at them for another second, then turned around and took off. Franks watched him go up the path and disappear into the darkness.

"Damn dog," Franks said, shaking his head. He then rushed around to the front of the car and took off, quickly getting out of the area. He had no idea if anyone was left, either friend or foe, but wasn't about to take chances.

Jacobs was near the corner of one of the back buildings, looking and waiting for a sign to indicate where Wickers was. Considering the car he came in was still parked in front of the maintenance building, Jacobs knew he was on foot somewhere. Now the question was Wickers waiting somewhere for him, or did he get away already? There were a couple rows of cars for sale in the back and Jacobs thought he might have been hiding in between one of them. He was just about to make a move when he heard something coming up behind him. He quickly turned to see what it was and jumped, thinking it may have been Wickers flanking him. Jacobs was relieved, though, to find out it was Gunner.

"What are you doing here?" Jacobs said. "You're supposed to be with the kids."

Gunner looked at him and tilted his head, making

a low noise as if he was talking back and saying no way.

"I think he's in there somewhere."

Gunner then let out a loud and deep bark.

"What? You sense him?"

Gunner then barked again, giving Jacobs the impression that the dog really could sense where he was.

"Gunner, get him."

The dog immediately took off like a rocket and sprinted in between the cars. Jacobs closely followed him, at least as much as he could. Gunner was moving at a frenetic pace between the cars and Jacobs couldn't keep up with him. After a minute and a few rows in, Jacobs heard the scream of a man who sounded like he just got attacked. He then heard Gunner growling. Jacobs raced around a few cars until he came to where the sounds were coming from. He got there in time to see Wickers on the ground, with Gunner's mouth deeply entrenched onto his arm. Wickers was actively trying to fight back, throwing a few punches at the top of the dog's head to get him to cut him loose. It wasn't doing him much good, though.

Wickers knew he was going to have to do something desperate to get the dog off of him. He looked around and saw the gun that he dropped when the dog lunged at him. It was only a few feet away. Trying to block the pain from his arm out of his mind, Wickers tried to drag himself along the pavement, with the weight of the dog slowing him down. Shooting and killing the dog was his only option. Jacobs saw the gun and knew what Wickers was trying to do. Just as Wickers was within reach of the weapon, Jacobs raced around them and kicked the gun away from his hand.

"Gunner, release."

The dog did as his owner requested and let go of Wickers' arm. He sat down in front of the man's legs and continued to growl at him. As Jacobs stood over his body, Wickers knew what was coming next. He was getting nervous and anxious, hoping he could do or say something to prevent it.

"Listen, let me go and I'll go to a new state. You'll never see me again."

Jacobs sighed. "That's the problem. I just don't believe anything you say."

"I'll never lift a finger against you again. I promise."

"Well, you just took three kids who are my family. I can't really forgive you for that or let you off the hook."

"Please, there must be something we can do to work this out. I'll, uh, I'll join up with you. I'll help you fight against Mallette. I've always hated him anyway."

Jacobs took a deep breath, knowing what he had to do. He didn't want to take another life, but he didn't see another way. If he let him get away, he'd always have to worry about him coming back and doing something else. Once on Mallette's payroll, always on Mallette's payroll. Jacobs didn't like killing anyone in general, but he especially didn't like doing it to someone who wasn't even armed. But then he thought about what Wickers did to those kids and the decision wasn't so hard.

"No hard feelings," Jacobs said, aiming his gun.

Jacobs then pumped Wickers' body with several rounds of lead, killing the man instantly. Jacobs stood there for a few seconds, staring at the dead man, realizing that this round against Mallette was over. He wound up victorious again. But there really wasn't a winner. Not when the kids would have a lifetime of bad memories from their encounter. He just hoped it wouldn't haunt them too much. Jacobs then called Gunner and started walking down the path toward the front gate.

"You did a good job tonight," Jacobs said.

Gunner looked at him and Jacobs could almost swear that the dog was smiling. He then barked.

"All right, you win. I know. I couldn't have done it without you. You get a steak dinner tonight."

Gunner barked again.

"You deserve it."

## 16

The following day, Jacobs showed up to his brother's house to check on the kids. Considering all they'd been through the previous couple of days, they were being kept home from school. Jacobs was there with Gunner, letting the kids play around with him. They seemed to take a liking to the dog, and Jacobs thought it was good for Gunner too. While Jacobs gave him some free time every day, it was good for Gunner to be around others and kids for his development.

"When'd you decide to get a dog?" Terry asked.

"I didn't, really. Just kind of found each other."

"Seems like a good dog."

"He is. Would've been a lot tougher to do this without him," Jacobs said.

"Plus, I'm sure he helps to keep you company."

"Yeah, I guess so."

"So, what should we do now?" Terry said. "About keeping the kids safe?"

"For the time being, just keep a close eye on them. Take them to school, pick them up, don't let them play out front without you being out there with them. Same with the back."

Terry sighed. "We gonna have to do that forever?"

"Just for a little while. They won't try it again."

"How can you be so sure?"

"They rarely do the same thing twice," Jacobs answered. "Besides that, there's honestly not a lot of them left. Whatever they try next, I'm sure it won't have anything to do with you. Just in case, though, you got my number. Don't hesitate to use it if you feel you have to."

"So, what are you gonna do? Just keep picking them off."

Jacobs looked at the kids playing with Gunner, his mind thinking back to his own kids. "If that's what it takes."

"Just be careful."

Jacobs smiled. "That's the plan."

"You know you can come around more often. Kids would love to see you more. And the dog, too."

"Not just yet. Not until this is over."

"You don't have to do it alone. You don't have to put the weight of the world on your back."

Jacobs nodded, though he never did respond. He stayed for about five more minutes before he and

Gunner took off. He then went to the pawn shop to hang out with Franks for a little while.

"Just wanted to let you know how much I appreciate you helping me out with everything," Jacobs said. "Picking the kids up, before at that office building, just helping in general. You've made things a lot easier for me."

"Well, shucks, do you want me to come over and give you a few smooches?"

Jacobs rolled his eyes. "Really?"

Franks laughed, not really knowing what else to say except something sarcastic. "Well, if you really wanna show your appreciation, I'd appreciate a few more dollars in my wallet."

Jacobs decided to play along and reached into his back pocket, pulling out his wallet. He took out some money and handed it to him. Franks showed no shame in taking it, eagerly counting how much was there. He then looked up at Jacobs, somewhat surprised at the amount.

"Four five-dollar bills? That's it? Twenty dollars? That's all I'm worth to you?" Franks said, feigning insult.

"Well, that's just a down payment on the next installment."

Franks' eyes lit up. "Oh yeah?"

"Next month I'll give you ten."

"Gee, thanks a lot," Franks said, putting the money

in his pocket. "So, where you figuring on striking them next?"

"I don't know yet. Gonna take a few days to figure it out. Map out who's left, try to get a fix on where everyone is. Take it from there."

"Just don't take too long. As soon as Mallette hears what happened, he'll put a new plan in place."

A devilish grin came over Jacobs' face. "I'm counting on it."

Franks looked confused, but also intrigued at the same time. "What exactly you got up your sleeve?"

～

Jacobs had once again arrived at Wiggins' office, knowing the lawyer would be meeting with his boss the following morning, right on schedule. He walked into the office, more calmly than usual. As soon as the secretary saw him, her shoulders slumped down. She put her hand out before he had a chance to say anything.

"I'll get him."

Jacobs smiled, amused that she had the routine down pat by now. "Thanks."

Only a few seconds after paging her boss, the door to the office opened, Wiggins standing in the doorway. He waved Jacobs in. After they both settled in the office, they sat down across from each other.

"I hope this is a little more pleasant than the usual times that you're in here," Wiggins said.

"Yeah. I just wanted to tell you personally that I appreciate your help in this. I know you didn't have to, even with the threats, and who knows how it would've turned out if you hadn't helped out like you did."

Wiggins nodded, appreciating the personal thank you. "I take it you've settled things to a satisfactory conclusion?"

"The kids are safe."

"Good. I'm glad to hear it. And of our other friends who were involved in the situation?"

"Gone," Jacobs said. "Never to be heard from again."

There was an uncomfortable silence for a minute as Wiggins wondered what else Jacobs had on his mind. Though he surmised it was possible that's all there was, he had a feeling there was something more that his visitor wanted discussed.

"So what else can I do for you?"

"I take it you're still meeting with Mallette tomorrow?" Jacobs asked.

"That would be correct."

"Does he know what happened yet? Or will he by the time you get there?"

"Informing him of situations like these are some of my responsibilities," Wiggins said. "Comes with the job."

"Kind of figured as much. You think you could give him a message from me?"

"As long as it doesn't involve too many vulgarities," Wiggins joked.

Jacobs laughed. "No, nothing quite like that. Just wanted to know if you could give him something for me."

"Bombs aren't allowed in the facilities."

Jacobs reached into his pocket and pulled out a folded piece of paper and put it on the desk. "Just a note."

Wiggins looked at both the note and Jacobs curiously, wondering what the note could have entailed. Jacobs could see that the lawyer was intrigued.

"You can read it if you want to make sure it's not laced with any poison or anything," Jacobs said.

"It is part of my duties to read any documents before passing them along to him." Wiggins picked up the paper and unfolded it, reading it very quickly. A wry smile came over his face. "He's not going to like this."

"I know."

"I don't know if taunting him like this is the best strategy."

"I think it is. He'll lose his cool and do something stupid. That's his way."

"Well, if that's what you want, I'll deliver it."

❧

Wiggins arrived at the prison the next morning, same time as always. He was sitting at their usual table when Mallette was brought in. The crime boss tried to read his lawyer's face as he approached the table to see if he was bringing good news or not. He was very hopeful that their latest plan would be successful. He wasted no time or words in getting down to it.

"So? Is it finished?" Mallette asked, plenty of hope in his voice.

"Yes. It is finished."

"Well?"

Wiggins always hated being the one to deliver bad news. "Jacobs is alive, the kids were returned home, and Wickers, along with the rest of the men, are all dead."

Mallette sighed and closed his eyes, hearing the worst possible news that could have been delivered. "How many men?"

Wiggins hesitated for a second before answering. "Twelve."

The lawyer could see his boss' face turning red with anger. "Twelve men dead. Twelve men. Why is it so hard to kill this man? I give out the proper plans, I have enough men, I hand out everything that is needed to eliminate this man, and still...still, we cannot get rid of him. Why? Why is this so hard?"

Wiggins shook his head. "I don't know. He's a much more formidable opponent than we realized. Instead of being crushed at the deaths of his family, he has used that as motivation, as fuel. He won't be stopped."

"He can be and he will be. We'll devise something that he can't escape from," Mallette said. "We have to. How many men do we have left?"

Wiggins rubbed around his mouth. "Ten."

Mallette looked despondent at hearing how little of an organization he had left. He'd almost forgotten how many men Jacobs had already taken out. "Ten? If this keeps up I won't have an organization or a business to come back to."

"Maybe it would be best to hold off on plans of taking him out for now. To wait until you're out of here and can rebuild the organization."

"No. He must be dealt with and he must be dealt with now. Whether I'm inside or outside. He must be eliminated. Nothing else matters right now."

"OK."

"Let me think on a plan," Mallette said. "We may have to use more of our friends in New York. It might take some extra cash, some bonuses, but that's OK. We'll do what we have to to put this chapter behind us and move on. When you come back next week, I should have something."

"As you wish. Oh, I almost forgot," Wiggins said, reaching into his briefcase and pulling out Jacobs' note. He put it down in front of his boss. "This is for you."

"What is it?"

"I believe a note from your adversary. It was shoved under the door to my office late last night."

Mallette looked disturbed, unsure what he was about to see, but positive it probably wouldn't be good. "Did you read it?"

"I have not. It was in an envelope that asked for it to be delivered to you. I did not look any further into it."

Mallette picked it up gingerly, almost afraid to read it. He opened it up and read it. It was only one line. One question.

"What else you got?" the note read.

Mallette quickly became enraged, angry that he was being taunted and mocked. "What else you got?" Mallette said. "What else you got?"

Mallette dropped the note back down on the table and stood up. Wiggins' eyes first went to the piece of paper, then at his boss, seeing that he was about to lose control.

"I'll show him what else I got," Mallette said angrily. "I'll show him."

Mallette's eyes drifted back down to the table and saw that question again. The rage flared up again inside him. Jacobs was taunting him with his organization's ineptitude in taking him out. Nobody taunted or mocked him like that. Nobody. Even if he was locked up.

"I'll show him what else I got," Mallette said, flipping the table over in anger.

Wiggins was about to try and get his boss under

control, but it was too late. Three guards had already rushed over and started to subdue him. They started dragging him away, forcefully, as he was kicking and screaming the entire way out the door.

"I'll show him what else I got," he yelled. "I'll show him. I'll kill him. I'll kill him."

Mallette's voice trailed off, Wiggins believing that his boss was officially starting to lose it. He'd never seen him act so enraged that it looked like he'd gone crazy. With their meeting cut abruptly short, Wiggins packed his things back up in his briefcase and left the facility. As he got in his car, he looked at the man in the passenger seat.

"How'd he take it?"

"Just like you thought he would," Wiggins answered. "Flipped over a table, got so mad some guards had to come in and restrain him to take him away."

Jacobs smiled. "I guess now I'm in control of things. For the first time, I now feel like I'm in his head instead of him being in mine."

"Well, I wouldn't get too overconfident if I were you. He's sure to have a plan to come back at you."

"I'm counting on it. And when he does, I'll be ready. And then I'll finally cripple his organization. And he'll have nothing left. And then... I'll have won."

# ABOUT THE AUTHOR

Mike Ryan lives in Pennsylvania with his wife, four children, and three dogs. He is always working on another book. Visit his website at www.mikeryanbooks.com to find out more about his books.

facebook.com/mikeryanauthor

instagram.com/mikeryanauthor

## ALSO BY MIKE RYAN

Continue reading with Book 4 of The Eliminator Series:

The Eliminator

Also by Mike Ryan:

The Silencer Series

The Cain Series

The Extractor Series

The Brandon Hall Series

The Ghost Series

The Last Job

A Dangerous Man

The Crew

Printed in Great Britain
by Amazon